"You're suggesting we . . . m-marry?"

Having stuttered the last word incredulously, Blythe shook her head in disbelief.

Finch smiled wryly. "That's the general idea. The courts would look more favorably upon my custody of Lief if I were married. I obviously need a wife."

"Was this Lief's idea?" Blythe hazarded tautly.

"Lief's?" There was nothing feigned in the look of surprise that crossed Finch's face. "Why on earth would you think that? Or don't you think I'm capable of choosing for myself who to marry?" He slanted her a lazily bantering glance that left her feeling breathless.

Blythe's mind reeled. Finch proposed the idea so calmly, so idly! Was this to be a marriage of convenience . . . or love?

Kerry Allyne developed wanderlust after emigrating with her family from England to Australia. A long working holiday enabled her to travel the world before returning to Australia where she met her engineer husband-to-be. After marriage and the birth of two children, the family headed north to Summerland, a popular surfing resort, where they run a small cattle farm and an electrical contracting business. Kerry Allyne's travel experience adds much to the novels she spends her days writing— when, that is, she's not doing company accounts or herding cattle!

Books by Kerry Allyne

HARLEQUIN ROMANCE

2647—TIME TO FORGET
2725—MERRINGANNEE BLUFF
2737—RETURN TO WALLABY CREEK
2761—STRANGER IN TOWN
2809—THE TULLAGINDI RODEO
2869—CARPENTARIA MOON
2929—LOSING BATTLE
2947—BENEATH WIMMERA SKIES

HARLEQUIN PRESENTS

743—LEGALLY BOUND
783—TROPICAL EDEN

Man of the High Plains

Kerry Allyne

Harlequin Books

TORONTO • NEW YORK • LONDON
AMSTERDAM • PARIS • SYDNEY • HAMBURG
STOCKHOLM • ATHENS • TOKYO • MILAN

Original hardcover edition published in 1988
by Mills & Boon Limited

ISBN 0-373-02990-X

Harlequin Romance first edition July 1989

CHAPTER ONE

WITH A SMILE Blythe Roberts said her last goodnight to her five-and-a-half-year-old nephew Lief, closed his bedroom door, and made her way back to the sitting room. He really was a most endearing child, she mused, and it was a great pity his mother—her sister Petra—had never seen fit to pay him enough attention to realise it. Now Petra would never have the chance to, for she had been killed in a water-skiing accident some six weeks ago, and once again her son had been left in the care of someone else.

Inside the sitting-room, Nathan Shearing, Blythe's boyfriend of some twelve months' standing, lifted his gaze from the television as she entered and seated herself on the sofa beside him. There was more than a hint of tiredness in her action, and as he noted it Nathan's lips tightened.

'So what do you intend doing about the boy?' he queried, both his question and his reference to Lief as 'the boy', as was his usual fashion, bringing a frown to Blythe's forehead. Only she was too weary tonight to take issue with him about the latter.

'In what way?' she merely countered instead, perplexed.

Nathan shrugged dismissively. 'Well, he's not

your child, is he?'

A whimsical smile touched the corners of Blythe's mouth. 'More often than not it feels as though he is!'

Certainly once Lief had begun crawling, and thus making more demands on his mother's time, Petra had begun to resent his presence even more deeply. The result being that she had increasingly left her sister and somewhat elderly mother to look after him. That burden had devolved even more on to Blythe when Lief's grandmother had succumbed to a particularly virulent form of 'flu when he was just three. Not that it had been entirely unexpected when Mrs Roberts had been found to have neither the strength, or perhaps the will, to fight the infection. She had never really recovered from the shock of her husband's sudden death in a chemical plant explosion some four years before. Why was it that death on so many occasions came in threes? Blythe had often found herself wondering.

'You still can't be expected to support him until he's fully grown,' Nathan went on to contend, bringing her back to the present.

Blythe's expression turned to one of surprise. 'I don't see why not. I do have care of him, after all.'

'But that's just it . . . you shouldn't have.' His tone became imbued with a slightly dogmatic inflection. 'Whether his father likes it or not, it really is his responsibility and it's about time he accepted some of it. When all's said and done, he's been allowed to get away so far without contributing a cent to the boy's upbringing.'

'Yes, but—well, I think Petra supposed he wouldn't be all that inclined to offer any support.' Blythe paused, her gaze dropping discomfitedly. 'She didn't exactly know Lief's father all that long.'

'All of one night, in fact, wasn't it?'

The badly scornful retort had Blythe hunching a deprecating shoulder, knowing full well Nathan's views regarding casual sex. Exercising self-control himself in that regard, he held little brief for those who didn't also do likewise.

'Something like that,' she hedged as a result.

'No, not something like that . . . precisely that, as I was given to understand it,' he promptly corrected, although in a more moderate tone. 'Nevertheless, she did still see fit to register the result of her night of presumed bliss in his father's name, and that being the case, I can see no reason, especially now, why he, or his family, shouldn't be called upon to assume responsibility for the boy.'

Blythe expelled a heavy breath. She had to admit she had often thought along somewhat similar lines herself. Lief's father *should* have been expected to contribute something—acknowledgement, support, just some of his time, even—to the rearing of his own son.

Simultaneously, though, she had to concede that Petra had never seemed to care whether Lief's father was even made aware of his responsibilities or not. But then Petra hadn't exactly cared much for Lief either when he began to make inroads into her freedom and enjoyment.

In fact, if it hadn't been for their mother

becoming very emotional when Petra suggested having an abortion—the idea coming so soon after her husband's death, Mrs Roberts hadn't been able to come to terms with even the thought of another—Blythe was sure her sister wouldn't have had Lief in the first place. But as it was, it appeared she had simply come to see her son as a means of obtaining her supporting mother's pension, which conveniently relieved her of the onus of having to work for a living.

'Yes—well . . .' she began slowly at length. 'She still really only knew his name and the general area he came from. I don't think she did ever know his actual address.'

'Although that could be solved quite easily, surely?' Nathan was quick to propose. 'Via the electoral rolls, for instance.'

'I—I suppose so,' Blythe faltered. 'Since Petra obviously was never interested in locating him, I've never given it much thought.'

'Although now that she's dead, circumstances are completely different, of course.'

Blythe's stomach constricted. 'You're saying you think I should try and get in touch with Lief's father?'

'Actually, I'm saying more than that,' Nathan confirmed her fear in decisive accents. Then, more softly, 'Look, I know how you've come to feel about the boy, but . . . he's not yours, Blythe, and to be quite honest . . . well, I think it's appropriate that his father should now take custody of him. No, let me finish,' he inserted swiftly when she would have protested. 'You know you've said yourself on occasion that it wasn't right that the boy's father should have been allowed to disregard so completely his part in the affair, and I truly believe now is the time to do something about it once and for all. In any case, when you and I have talked about our marrying, I'm sure you never contemplated—and I definitely didn't—our starting life together with—well, not to put too fine a point on it, another man's unwanted offspring along for company.' Pausing, he took a deep breath, his voice firming with conviction when he continued, 'If this man wants to go around siring children then he should be prepared to accept the consequences of his actions, because I'm sorry, but I for one am *not* prepared to pay the price for his indiscretions! I fail to see why I should and, quite frankly, I don't see why you should either! Hell, you've as good as been the boy's mother for the last five years, but now I consider it's more than past time for his own father to take over. After all, the boy's not a Roberts, and he certainly isn't a Shearing. He's a Carmody. That's what he was registered as, that's what he's called, and that's what I believe he should now actually become!'

Blythe gasped. 'You mean you want me to— just give him up?' She gave a rejecting shake of her head. 'I might never see him again!'

'I don't see why. You could always visit him . . . just as you would have done when he'd remained with Petra after we had married,'

Nathan was swift to remind her.

'But that would have been different,' she defended urgently. 'She was my sister; I knew her, and Lief would still have been living in Geelong. His father comes from the high country, almost a day's drive away.' And as more arguments came to mind, 'Besides, he might be married himself by now, and—and refuse to even admit that Lief could be his child! Or, after all this time, not even believe Lief *is* his, if it comes to that!'

'Although he *is* the registered father . . . and these days they do have tests that can prove these things conclusively, don't they?'

Blythe's mouth shaped ironically. 'Although only provided the person concerned is willing to undergo them, I should imagine.'

Undeterred, Nathan went on almost immediately. 'Well, be that as it may, for all you know he may be quite prepared to accept the boy, anyway. In fact, once he's seen him he may not even be in a position to dispute paternity.'

A frown drew Blythe's arched brows together. 'What makes you say that?'

'His distinctive colouring for a start,' he supplied unhesitatingly. 'I mean, it's obvious he didn't get those predominantly green eyes and that jet-black hair from your side of the family, did he?'

No, he was right there, Blythe once again had to concede. Petra had been a blue-eyed blonde, and certainly Lief hadn't resembled anyone else in her small family, either in complexion or feature.

'I guess not,' she had little choice but to allow,

albeit reluctantly. 'But, oh . . . I don't want to give him up, Nathan. There's more to it than mere responsibility. I love him, and he's become part of me even if he isn't mine.'

Nathan exhaled heavily. 'But he isn't part of me,' he stated explicitly. 'And as I said . . . I'm sorry, but I refuse to bear the burden for someone else's sexual indulgence.'

Blythe chewed at her lower lip. She supposed he had a point, although at the same time . . . 'But what if his father won't acknowledge him, or—or he's not the type of person to make a suitable parent? I couldn't possibly agree to it if I thought Lief wasn't going to be happy; if he wasn't going to be loved and wanted, and well treated.'

'Except that it's also just as possible the reverse could apply,' Nathan promptly proposed with a reasonableness she found herself fighting against accepting. 'For all you're aware, his father may be quite prepared to accept him, and even be able to offer him considerably more than you can. For instance, if, as you say, his father comes from the high country, then I guess there's a possibility that he, or his family, could own land. Land that the boy is rightfully entitled to lay claim to, perhaps. And if that is the case, then it's an inheritance I'm sure you wouldn't wish to deprive the boy of . . . just because you let your own feelings get in the way of his best interests.'

'That's not true!' Blythe burst out resentfully. 'And nor have you a shred of evidence to prove Lief might be entitled to anything!'

'And by refusing to investigate the possibility, you're hoping that's the way it will stay, is that it?' he countered immediately in subtle tones.

'No! I would never deliberately try to prevent Lief from benefiting from anything, and I think you're being grossly unfair by implying that I would!'

'Although only because I also want what's best for us too,' Nathan tried to impress on her, catching hold of her hand. 'And starting our marriage with someone else's offspring in tow is not my idea of being in our best interests. If we support any children, I want them to be ours, that's all.' His blue eyes sought hers persuasively. 'Is that so wrong? I mean, it's not as if he's *your* child even—and who's to say his father won't love him as much as you do? At least we owe it to him to give him the opportunity, don't you think?'

In truth, Blythe wasn't quite sure just what to think. From having been railing against the man for evading his responsibilities, Nathan was now seeming to imply that he was deserving of their consideration, and she could only stare at him in distracted confusion.

Apparently taking her silence for agreement, Nathan continued, 'So I'll start checking the electoral rolls tomorrow, OK? Now, what was his first name again?'

'Price . . . Price Carmody,' she supplied automatically, still a little dazed, and not only by his sudden change in attitude, but also by the speed with which it was all happening. The matter had never even been mentioned previously, and yet now . . . Now decisions were being made before she had really had a chance to think them over.

'And have you any idea whereabouts in the high country he came from? It covers a wide area, after all, and it would help if we could narrow it down to some degree.'

Blythe ran a hand through her hair and sighed resignedly. 'Oh, somewhere around Omeo, I think.' A frown of concentration made an appearance. 'The Yuroka Valley, I believe Petra once said.'

Nathan nodded in satisfaction. 'Well, that should help considerably.' He paused, an encouraging half-smile touching his lips as he took in her worried features: the troubled grey eyes, the serious cast to her generous mouth, the feathered bob of russet-coloured hair now tousled by her agitated fingers. 'And stop looking so apprehensive, huh? It will turn out for the best, you'll see.'

Blythe only wished she felt the same. 'But what if Lief doesn't want to go, Nathan? I can't just dump him and . . .'

'No, of course you can't,' he was quick to interpose. 'But at the same time, who's to say he'll be a problem? Children are extremely adaptable creatures, you know . . . and they forget very swiftly as well. So let's cross that bridge if and when we come to it, hmm? For now, I'll simply see about locating his father's whereabouts and, if I'm successful, we'll drive up to see him at the weekend.'

'We? This weekend?' she was startled into exclaiming.

'Well, of course,' he returned in surprised tones. 'There's no time like the present, and we are *both* involved, when all's said and done. Besides, you'd surely like some moral support, at least, when you see this man, wouldn't you?'

'I—I guess so,' she conceded, if a touch doubtfully on abruptly finding herself unsure as to whether he was offering to accompany her for her benefit or his own. 'Although to be truthful, I wasn't really anticipating going there, in any event. I was merely thinking of writing to him, initially.'

Nathan shook his head in a decisive gesture. 'No, I'm positive going in person is the only way to handle this matter. It will doubtless be more productive done face to face. Apart from letters stringing the matter out for God knows how long, it's too easy to answer in the negative from a distance.'

'You're probably right,' Blythe was forced to own, despite being unable to stop herself from wondering if his main concern wasn't merely the prevention of that negative being uttered.

Two evenings later, Nathan arrived to tell Blythe that he had found the information they needed.

'According to the rolls the whole area seems peopled with nothing *but* Carmodys—or at least, them and Haddons—but there was a Price Carmody among them . . . and from the Yuroka Valley, as you thought,' he relayed in a satisfied manner.

Blythe's feelings on hearing his news were nowhere near as straightforward, however. On the one hand, she could understand and even sympathise with Nathan's feelings on the matter, but on the other, she dreaded the prospect of Lief's disappearing out of her life. Simultaneously, she was also conscious tht if there was the smallest chance of Lief's father being able to offer him an advantage she couldn't—as Nathan had suggested —then there was no way she would ever do anything to prevent her nephew from obtaining any such benefit.

Thus, when at Nathan's insistence, they set off for the foothills of Victoria's alpine region early the following Saturday morning, Blythe was in a more or less resigned frame of mind. It was merely an investigative trip, after all, and no harm could come from that, surely?

They had left Lief with a next-door neightbour who also had a child much his age, and with whom he would stay overnight, because it was too far for them to return that day. Actually, Nathan had wanted to take Lief with them—together with all his belongings, Blythe had begun to suspect in some shock—seemingly intent on relieving them of her nephew's presence as soon as possible. But in that regard Blythe had been the one to put her foot down. Not only had she considered it inadvisable for Lief to be present at any such initial investigation concerning his future, but she fully intended to ensure there was more than one meeting before any decision, either way, was even contemplated.

They finally arrived at Yuroka, the small township in the valley, about three in the afternoon, and after stopping in order to seek information as to just where in the valley they might locate Price Carmody, they continued on.

'So he does own land . . . just as I reasoned,' commented Nathan with evident pleasure, making reference to their recent advice that Price Carmody's farm was at the head of the valley. 'And land that would certainly be well worth owning, by the look of it.' A slightly envious note entered his voice.

Looking about her at the thickly grassed valley with its scattering of homesteads, at the densely wooded surrounding hills and ridges, and the burbling river the road ran beside, its waters turning silver beneath the slanting rays of the sun, Blythe was prepared to concede that he was probably right—but with a proviso.

'Although only if one *wanted* to live on the land,' she couldn't refrain from qualifying somewhat sharply. He seemed to be implying that material assets were all that mattered!

'Meaning?' Nathan flashed her a narrowed look.

Blythe eyed him back resolutely. 'Merely that farming isn't to everyone's liking . . . and that, to date, Lief hasn't ever exhibited any great penchant for outdoor activities, even!'

'Mmm, but then has that been by choice . . . or circumstances?'

'And just what's that supposed to imply?' it was

her turn to query tightly now.

Nathan shook his head. 'Oh, don't get all prickly about it. I wasn't having a shot at you.' His mouth shaped sardonically. 'Who knows better than I do all that you've done for the boy? Nevertheless, that doesn't alter the fact that Petra never did much to encourage him in any activity, either inside or out, and while you do your best, the free time you do have out of working hours is still mostly taken up cleaning and tidying the house, cooking washing and ironing, and other such necessary chores. Hell, even you and I never seem able to go anywhere any more!'

'Well, it's hard enough to find the money to send Lief to a child care centre every day now, without paying for baby-sitters as well!' retorted Blythe defensively. 'While as for the other . . . all I can say is, Lief's certainly never shown any discontent or—or recalcitrance regarding his life-style.'

'Which, in a way, really only serves to prove *my* point!' he astounded her somewhat by suddenly declaring. 'Because he's such a—placid child, then I've no doubt he'll take to farming life with equal docility.' He uttered an ironic half-laugh. 'Lord, why wouldn't he? If only for the fact that a farm has an abundance of those creatures that *all* children love being around . . . namely, animals!'

He seemed to have an answer for everything, and Blythe pressed her lips together vexedly. Yet neither could she claim his theory was altogether wrong in Lief's case either, because her nephew had expressed a wish for a puppy of his own on a couple of occasions. A wish that she had reluctantly had to refrain from granting because it would not only have been just another expense to add to her already stretched budget, but also because she hadn't thought it fair that any animal should have to spend the majority of its life confined to a small backyard on its own.

Moreover, she had also taken exception to the emphasis Nathan had seemed to place on his description of Lief as placid and docile. He had made him sound as if he was insipid and somehow lacking in character, whereas she was well aware nothing could have been further from the truth. Lief merely liked to please, that was all, and personally she considered he had displayed a great inner strength over the years in the way he had come to terms with his own mother's obvious lack of interest in him.

'That must be the place up there.'

Nathan's comment abruptly returned Blythe's thoughts to the immediate and, as she realised they had reached the end of the bitumen and were now travelling on a much narrower, hard-packed dirt road, the hills bounding the valley beginning to converge, her gaze quickly encompassed both the gateway she could see a short distance ahead and the homestead that Nathan was indicating, which was nestled among some trees at the base of the hill on their right.

'I guess so,' she allowed with a sigh. 'I can't see another house further along, and the road's becoming narrower all the time. It looks as if it probably peters out altogether behind that ridge ahead.'

Nodding his agreement, Nathan turned in over the cattle grid that gave on to the property. Following the track that led up to the homestead, he brought their vehicle to a halt outside the wire fence that surrounded the large and solidly constructed, veranda-lined building, their arrival bringing forth three or four barking cattle dogs from behind a nearby shed.

Alighting, Blythe patted the dogs cautiously, then on looking about her swallowed tautly, wishing she was back in Geelong. But when Nathan, without further ado, immediately pushed open the gate in the fence and went striding towards the house, she had little option but to follow him.

However, when their knocking elicited no response, nor their ensuing exploration of the many outbuildings, she was nowhere near as displeased by their inability to locate anyone as Nathan evidently was.

'Oh, that's just great!' he burst out frustratedly as they returned to the front of the house. 'We drive all this way and the bloody place is deserted! God, we might have to wait hours before someone comes!'

'They—he could even be away . . . on holidays, or something, I suppose,' put forward Blythe, not unhopefully, and received a scowling glare for her efforts.

'No, the girl in the shop would have said something if that had been the case,' Nathan dismissed the idea out of hand. 'In small places like this everyone always knows what everyone else is doing. No, it seems we've no choice but to just wait, twiddling our thumbs, until . . .' He broke off, cocking to his head to one side as the sound of an engine abruptly began throbbing in the warm air. 'Where's that coming from? It doesn't sound all that far away.'

'No, just a little further along the road, I think,' Blythe acceded. 'Past those trees on the other side, perhaps.'

'And it could be just the man we're looking for,' poroposed Nathan eagerly, already starting towards the car. 'Or, if not, then we might at least be able to discover Price Carmody's exact whereabouts.'

A distinct possibility, Blythe supposed as she followed him—although with somewhat less enthusiasm.

Back in the vehicle again, Nathan headed down to the gateway and then turned on to the dirt road once more, following it past the trees Blythe had mentioned, and peering over the dry and yellow, waist-high grass that lined its length in an effort to locate the source of the noise they had heard.

Then suddenly they came upon a wide, fenced paddock where someone on a tractor was methodically baling hay, and leaving the car near the open gateway they made their way into the field in order to attract the man's attention.

It still took a while before he completed the wind-row he was working on, but finally the tractor and the baler it trailed were brought to a halt beside them, although the man neither cut the ignition nor dismounted, but merely sat surveying them idly and waited for them to speak.

On obtaining his first clear look at the man, however, Nathan promptly muttered a satisfied exclamation in a triumphant undertone, and even Blythe's breath caught in her throat as she noticed just how similar were his features to those of her nephew. He possessed the same almost jet-black hair, judging by that just visible beneath the wide-brimmed hat he was wearing, the same warm complexion—only his was deeply tanned—the same shapely mouth, but in this case more firmly moulded and with a promise of both strength and humour.

Only a couple of differences stood out. Although both had the same long, sable lashes, this man's eyes were a pure green, whereas Lief's were tinged with hazel. As well, as Blythe estimated, he was only a little over thirty, not surprisingly the lines and planes of the face before her were leaner and more masculinely defined, the well-cut jaw firmer and somehow suggestive of an unyielding streak.

Quickly recovering from the surprise the man's appearance had created, Blythe now moved closer to ensure she was heard over the sound of the tractor.

'Mr Carmody . . . ?' she enquired a trifle tentatively even so, and he nodded briefly in affirmation.

'We're here about your son!' Nathan immediately advised in peremptory tones, apparently arbitrarily deciding that he should be their spokesman. 'He's over five years old now, and we think it's time you took responsibility for him instead of expecting others to do it for you!'

CHAPTER TWO

HER COMPANION'S censuring outburst had Blythe turning to him, aghast.

'Nathan . . . !' she started to remonstrate discomfitedly, but was prevented from adding anything further by Carmody's intervention.

'Is that so?' he countered on a highly sardonic note. 'Well, I'm sorry to disappoint you, but I don't know what the hell you're talking about . . . because I don't happen to have a son.'

'Well, at least not one you've to date acknowledged siring, that's for sure!' Nathan was swift to retort contemptuously. 'None the less, you needn't think of fob us off with claims of not knowing about it, because the facts speak for themselves! The boy's a dead ringer for you, and that's something you can't dispute. So what have you got to say about that?'

Carmody gave an uninterested shrug, the bronzed muscles of his broad shoulders, revealed by his tank top, rippling powerfully.

'Nothing much, except that you're wasting my time.' His voice began to harden. 'And neither should you think you're going to lay the blame at my door due to some kind of *alleged* similarity, just because your—um—little friend here,' a scathing glance was cast in Blythe's direction, 'ended up with something she didn't want! I'm afraid you've picked the wrong man to try and pull that stunt on. For a start, I'm thankful to say, I've never even seen her before!' A dismissive look now followed the first.

'No, I know you haven't seen me before,' Blythe herself confirmed quickly, placatingly, and before Nathan could do any more damage. God, it was a discussion they needed to have with the man, surely, not a confrontation! 'But it's not a stunt, Mr Carmody, and—and nor is Lief my child. He's my sister's. Unfortunately she's dead now, though, and . . .'

'As we want to get married . . .' Nathan cut in, only to be interrupted himself.

'You want to dump this unwanted kid on to whoever you can deceive into acknowledging him, is that it?' Carmody derided.

'No, that's not it!' Blythe denied vehemently, both taking exception to his interpretation and annoyed with Nathan for having engendered it. 'If simply getting rid of Lief was all that interested me, I could put him up for adoption, or put him in a home. We—I—just thought that—that if his father would agree to take him, it would be more suitable.'

A dark brow arched expressively. 'For the kid . . . or the pair of you?'

'What does it matter?' interjected Nathan in a pugnacious vein. 'Naturally, when we have a child we want it to be our own, not someone else's bastard!'

'*Nathan!*' gasped Blythe in a mixture of shock and anger. He had never spoken of Lief in such a manner before, and what was more, she hardly thought it likely to do their present cause much good either!

'Well, he is, whether you like me calling a spade a spade or not,' he defended, although he did at least have the grace to look a little discomfited, she noted. 'Although that isn't really the point, in any case,' he added swiftly. 'The point is, he *should* be his father's responsibility, not ours!'

'Then I suggest you find the father as soon as possible . . . for the boy's sake, if no one else's!' put in Carmody succinctly.

Nathan's chin became more outthrust as he gazed up at the man eyeing him with such scorn. 'Oh, don't try giving us that! As you very well know, we've already found him!' Pausing, he indicated the still reverberating engine of the tractor irately. 'And can't you turn that damned thing off? I don't intend to keep shouting in order to make myself heard!'

'Then you'll doubtless be pleased to know you won't have to, because *I* don't intend sitting here much longer. I've heard just about all I want to, thanks!'

'Oh, yeah? Well, we didn't just pick this place with a pin, you know. We knew who to look for, and where! The boy's a Carmody all right, and it's time you acknowledged him as such!'

'And all because—according to you—I happen to

look like him to some degree?' An ironic laugh
issued from Carmody's bronzed throat. 'That's
hardly what I would call evidence, conclusive or
otherwise, of any particular involvement on my
part when there are dozens of Carmodys in this
district. All of whom, I might add, have descended
from the one family, so that a certain similarity of
appearance, and even a repetition of names, isn't
uncommon around here.'

Nathan allowed himself the satisfaction of a
mocking smile. 'Although fortunately—or unfortunately for you—there was only one *Price* Carmody
listed on the electoral rolls for this district!'

'Price Carmody!' Momentarily, the other man
looked slightly taken aback, and then his expression
hardened, a muscle beginning to twitch in his
cheek. 'Then you really have got the wrong
man—and in more ways than one—haven't you?'
he bit out savagely.

Unsure as to the meaning of that insertion,
Blythe still frowned and bit her lip as she digested
the import of his initial words.

'You mean you're—not Price Carmody?' she all
but gulped.

He nodded sharply. 'That's right.'

'Th-then who . . . ?'

'Oh, of course he is,' broke in Nathan to claim
impatiently. 'Don't let him fool you with a trick
like that. You're forgetting that he's already
admitted his name is Carmody, *and* that the girl in
the shop told us the last property along this road
was where we would find him.'

'Except that this doesn't happen to be the last property,' Carmody advised him coldly. 'There's another beyond that spur.' He nodded towards the tree-covered ridge that descended into the valley a short distance away.

Blythe swallowed. 'And—and that's where . . . ?'

'My almost *sixty*-year-old uncle, Price Carmody, lives.'

'Sixty!' she repeated involuntarily. 'Oh, but he can't be!'

'We've only *his* word for it that he is,' scorned Nathan.

All of a sudden, it seemed to Blythe as if an almost expectant hush had fallen over the valley, and then she realised why. Carmody had at last turned the tractor off, was even dismounting, and her mouth abruptly went dry as she watched him jump agilely to the ground.

He was taller than she had supposed, she noticed inconsequentially—a good couple of inches more than Nathan's five feet ten, at least. He was also broad of chest and lithe of waist; his legs, cased in snug-fitting jeans, long and muscular.

But it was the look on his strikingly masculine face—bleak and ominous—that had caused her sudden feeling of trepidation, and increased it now as he came to stand before Nathan with his long, blunt and obviously strong fingers resting on lean hips in a stance that was at once self-assured and challenging.

'Are you calling me a liar?' he demanded in a deadly tone.

There was a moment's hesitation and then, to Blythe's despair and vexation, Nathan's mouth pursed obstinately. 'And if I am?'

'Then I wouldn't recommend it!' came the steel-edged retort. 'Nor would I recommend you attempt to confront my uncle with this far-fetched accusation of yours either, because for your information he happens to have three grown sons who, I can assure you, are likely to react to the preposterous suggestion of any infidelity on his part with considerably less restraint than I have to present!'

'Meaning, they're as willing to abdicate their responsibilities as . . .'

'Nathan! Will you please shut up—for just one moment!' Blythe interrupted furiously, hastily—to his surprise and evident resentment—but beginning to lose patience with him altogether now. Couldn't he sense the antagonism he was creating? Or was it that he simply didn't care, so long as he made his own thoughts known? She turned to the other man with an apologetic glance.

'Look, I'm sorry for the original misunderstanding, Mr Carmody, and—and of course we won't be accusing your uncle. In fact, it was never my intention to accuse anyone of anything. We're—I'm merely trying to locate Lief's father, that's all, and since Price Carmody was the name my sister registered as being that of his father . . .' She shrugged meaningly.

'And hasn't it yet occurred to you that she might just have got it wrong?' he countered in satirical accents, and although Blythe didn't strictly appre-

ciate his mockery, she was at least relieved to note
that his earlier open hostility appeared to have
dissipated slightly.

Or it had, until Nathan promptly scoffed,
'Hardly, when the boy's as good as your double!'

The antipathy that immediately emanated from
Carmody was almost palpable, and once again
Blythe rushed to defuse the situation. 'Oh, please
. . . I have some photographs here that I took of
Lief a couple of months ago. If—if you would just
look at them I'm sure you'll be able to understand
our—position a little better,' she stammered as she
began searching about in her shoulder bag. A
sudden thought sprang to mind. 'Or—or, as you
said a repetition of names wasn't uncommon
around here, perhaps you would know of another
Price Carmody, who may even have moved from
this area during the last few years, but who could
be the person we're looking for. Someone who
would be approaching thirty now, or something
like that age, I guess, and who was in Lorne for the
New Year festivities some six years ago.' She gazed
up at him hopefully as she held out an envelope
containing half a dozen photographs.

Carmody made no move to accept them,
however. 'Lorne?' he queried intently instead, his
own glance narrowing.

Blythe nodded. 'You think you might know who
it could be?' she hazarded.

He didn't reply, but he did take the photographs
from her now, and proceeded to scan them slowly.
And as he perused each succeeding one his expres-

sion seemed to tighten, until at the last a succinct expletive appeared to escape him uncontrollably.

'Well, it's not me the boy's the double of, I can tell you that,' he quipped on a somewhat roughened note, replacing the photos in the envelope and returning them to Blythe.

'Although you do know who he does very closely resemble,' she deduced quietly.

He expelled a heavy breath. 'Uh—huh!' There was a brief pause before he revealed, 'My younger brother—Danny.' He paused again. 'Price Daniel Carmody.'

Behind her, Blythe heard Nathan utter an incredulous snort. 'You mean you're expecting us to believe that you yourself have a brother called Price, and yet it didn't occur to you that that's who we might be looking for?'

Carmody's mouth levelled. 'In view of the fact that he was never known as anything but Danny, around here at least, and since the name Price wasn't even mentioned until five minutes ago, no, I didn't immediately connect the two! Before that you were busily occupied contending that *I* was the boy's father . . . remember?' He raised a mocking brow.

The younger man's nostrils flared. 'And I wouldn't be at all surprised if . . .'

'Oh, be quiet, Nathan!' Blythe rounded on him with some asperity. What on earth was the matter with him? She had never seen him act this way before! She glanced back at Carmody doubtfully. 'You said . . . your brother *was* never known as anything but Danny,' she prompted.

He dipped his head briefly, his jaw suddenly tensing. 'He was killed in a car crash some six years ago . . . on his way back from Lorne.'

Shock sucked in Blythe's breath. 'I'm sorry,' she just managed to get out while she tried desperately to reconcile her stunned brain and emotions to the fact that her nephew really was totally parentless now.

'How do we know that's the truth, anyway?' put in Nathan suspiciously, but in a more judiciously whispered aside to Blythe on this occasion. 'He could just be covering up for his brother, who's moved elsewhere in the mean time.'

She shook her head thoughtfully. 'No, a claimed death would be too easy to prove or disprove, and if it was a cover-up, then why mention him in the first place?' she countered in a similar undertone. 'We didn't even know of his brother's existence until then.'

'Hmm . . .' He pondered the matter momentarily, and then with a somewhat grudging shrug of dismissal, redirected his attention to the man facing them, his next words being delivered at a more normal pitch. 'Well, that still makes you as closely related to the boy as anyone . . . and therefore as obligated to take custody of him and bear the responsibility and expense of his upbringing.'

Carmody's mouth curved disparagingly. 'And that's all that matters to you, isn't it? Finding someone, anyone, to foist the kid on to simply in order to get him out of your own lives, and completely irrespective of whether that person would make a suitable guardian or not, at that!' He shook his head in disgust. 'You're a disgrace, and I hate to think what the poor kid's life must have been like to date in your company! I'm merely surprised you haven't considered touting him round the whole valley seeking the highest bidder!'

Obviously unperturbed by the condemnation, Nathan simply gave an unconcerned shrug, but guessing she too had been included in the remarks, Blythe coloured with a mortified flush.

'That's unfair!' she defended huskily. 'You have no right to insinuate that we would be prepared to—to auction him off. W-we just thought locating his father and—and his family would be the best solution since—it won't be possible for him to remain with me for much longer. And that's much to my regret, not r-relief!' Her voice caught on a knot of grief that lodged in her throat and she had to struggle to displace it before continuing. 'What's more, naturally I intended to satisfy myself that—that if an agreement was reached concerning Lief coming here, then it would only be if there was someone suitable to take custody of him. I might add, I also meant to ensure he was quite amenable to the idea as well.'

'Oh?' He flicked a brow expressively high, clearly still less than convinced. 'And just how did you intend to achieve all that? With one afternoon's hurried meeting, and a glowing account for the boy about how you'd found someone who was willing to actually make him feel welcome in their home?'

Blythe gasped, but before she could speak Nathan interjected to disclose on an exasperated note, 'If I'd had my way we would have brought him with us today, and then the whole matter could have been settled here and now.'

'And as far as I'm concerned, your part in this *is* finished, as of right this minute!' grated Carmody, his expression implacable. 'I don't know who the hell you are—or even why you're here, if it comes to that—but I've listened to about as much as I'm able to from you! So why don't you just take a hike, sport, before you push me into forgetting there's a female present!'

Nathan drew himself up indignantly to his full height. 'Because it is due to Blythe's presence that I'm here! It's her interests that concern me, not yours—or any other member of your family's,' he added significantly. 'And in those interests I mean to remain here, whether you like it or not!'

The hard set of Carmody's mouth, the dangerously inflexible line of his posture, and the sudden awareness that each man had apparently taken an instant dislike to the other—perhaps even on sight—had Blythe swallowing in dismay and hastily holding out a restraining hand.

'No . . . please!' she entreated urgently of the taller man, surprising herself that she should have spontaneously sought forbearance from him rather than Nathan. Then, catching hold of her companion's arm, she surreptitiously began edging him away as she attempted to pacify with quiet persuasiveness, 'It's all right, really, Nathan. I know you're only doing what you think is best for me, but since Mr Carmody unfortunately does seem to—er—aggravate you somewhat . . .'

'That's the understatement of the year!' He case a baleful look over his shoulder. 'The obstructive, sarcastic bastard!'

Deeming it best to ignore his comments, Blythe continued in the same soothing vein as before. 'Then don't you think it might be in *our* best interests,' stressed deliberately, 'if you did perhaps return to the car, and just let me finish discussing the matter with him. I mean, I'm sure you would really prefer not to have anything more to do with him.'

His mouth curled. 'Isn't that the truth! But are you sure you'll be able to manage without my assistance?'

Implying that she was incapable of making the right decision without him being present! Blythe surmised with a spurt of bristling anger, but which she valiantly quelled. Now was patently not the time to express her feelings on that particular subject!

'Well, I could always call you over again if I did feel in need of your opinion,' she proposed tactfully in lieu.

'Mmm, I suppose there's always that option,' consideringly. He exhaled slowly. 'Well, if you're certain . . . I guess even if Carmody does manage to talk you into something I'm not in favour of, I could always change it afterwards.'

Blythe didn't comment. She merely smiled, if

through slightly gritted teeth, but still managing to convey agreement, and watched for a brief moment as he started for the car, before making her own way back to the tractor.

'So you actually managed to persuade him your best interests were more likely to be served without him around, did you?' drawled Carmody on a mocking note.

Still simmering as a result of Nathan's last comment, Blythe found nothing appeasing in either the content or the satire of the remark. Rather, it simply succeeded in exacerbating her temper, especially on her recollecting his previous supposition which had indirectly led to his last dispute with Nathan.

'That's none of your business!' she flared. 'Nor, might I add, do you have any business in casting unfounded aspersions on my treatment of Lief! I've done nothing *but* care for that child ever since he was born, the last two years almost single-handedly, and I'm not having you claiming otherwise just because you've suddenly learnt of his existence, or you might just find I'm disinclined to allow you to even see him, let alone . . .' She broke off with a gulp on abruptly finding her jaw spanned by a strong, hard hand, and a pair of dangerously glinting green eyes not far distant from her own.

'Don't threaten me, sweetheart!' Carmody warned in a low voice that was all the more menacing because of its very softness. 'I don't take kindly to people who try to stand over me.' He paused, his expression altering again in a split instant as a lazy tilt suddenly caught at one corner of his shapely mouth. 'Not even when it's a female who's as easy on the eye as you are.' He drew his fingers along the line of her jaw in a long, slow stroke that shocked Blythe with the unexpected sensations of awareness and breathlessness it aroused.

Flushed and flustered, she immediately took a quick step backward. Nathan had never had such a disruptive physical effect on her. But then maybe that unexpected compliment had had something to do with it, she decided. It had been a long time since Nathan had commented on her appearance, in any fashion. And after all, it wasn't even as if this man was the kind that normally appealed to her. She preferred them not quite so self-contained, so invulnerable, so . . . overpoweringly male!

'I—well . . .' she began unsteadily, and much to her annoyance, so that she purposely halted, took a steadying breath, and resolutely started again. 'You shouldn't have alleged that my only interest concerning Lief was in getting rid of him!'

'Then perhaps you should have taken the time to explain the matter more fully before rushing to jump to your own conclusions,' he wasn't above retorting meaningfully, and Blythe bent her head in self-conscious acknowledgement of his point. 'So just who are you, anyway, for a start?' he added in somewhat dry accents.

Doing her best to ignore the inherent mockery in his tone, Blythe strove to recover her composure and replied as matter-of-factly as possible, 'My name's Roberts—Blythe Roberts—and I live in Geelong.' Her head tilted, brows lifting. 'And you . . . ?'

'Finch Carmody,' he supplied with a twist to his lips that bordered on taunting. 'My house is a couple of hundred yards back that way,' nodding towards town, 'on the other side of the road.'

'The large sandstock brick place with the white-painted, geometric-patterned rail enclosing the veranda?' she detailed, wanting to ensure there were no further misunderstandings.

'That's the one,' the confirmation came cursorily. 'And now that the amenities have finally been settled . . .' He paused, his green gaze became watchful. 'You said you had always cared for the boy, and almost single-handedly for the last couple of years . . . yet the impression you gave originally was that his mother had only recently died.'

'And so she did. Six weeks ago, to be precise,' Blythe averred, wondering irrelevantly why his calling Lief 'the boy' didn't grate with her as it did when Nathan said the same.

'Then why so much responsibility apparently falling on you? Was she in poor health, or something?' Finch Carmody persisted.

Blythe stirred uncomfortably beneath his unwavering glance. She had hoped to have avoided such explanations, but it appeared Finch Carmody was just too alert to what had already been said, not to mention clearly suspicious of it, to allow any evasion now.

'I'm afraid Petra was a—a somewhat—indifferent

mother,' she disclosed reluctantly, but attempting to minimise her sister's attitude all the same.

'In other words, she didn't want him either!'

His last word had Blythe's chin immediately angling higher as she sensed more criticism of herself. 'Either doesn't come into it . . . as I thought I'd already explained!' she snapped rancorously. 'No one could love Lief more than I do, and there's no way I would even have contemplated being parted from him if it hadn't been for—for . . .'

'Your fiancé's disliking him so intensely?' put in Finch with biting derision.

Blythe inhaled sharply. 'He does not dislike him intensely! He merely doesn't feel inclined to pay the price for someone else's irresponsibility, that's all! And just to put the record straight—to show how wrong you are on all counts—nor is he my fiancé.'

Finch shrugged imperturbably. 'Well, lover, then, if that's what you prefer.'

'He's not that either!' she denied on a simmering note. 'He, at least, believes in exercising some discipline over *his* sexuality!' A caustic edge made its way into her voice. 'As it so happens, we simply have an—an understanding concerning our marrying—not that I can see what that has to do with you, in any event.'

'Except in so far as it affects my nephew, of course.'

So he was prepared to acknowledge Lief as such. Blythe was unsure whether her strongest feeling was relief, or depression, at the idea.

'Meaning you're considering accepting him, then? Of—of applying to the authorities for custody of him?' she sounded on a taut breath.

Finch uttered a short, humourless laugh. 'Sweetheart, considering the child's similarity of features to my brother, the dovetailing of Danny's whereabouts at the time with those of your sister, *and* in view of what I've heard this afternoon, you couldn't stop me doing so now, even if you wanted to!' he declared, leaving her in no doubt as to his intentions. 'The Carmodys have always taken care of their own, and certainly Danny's son deserves a damn sight better than having to suffer the callous rejection, and doubtless disparagement, of *that* miserable, self-centred toad!' He made a contemptuous gesture in Nathan's direction.

All too aware that her companion hadn't exactly covered himself in glory that afternoon, Blythe could only lift a deprecatory shoulder and offer faintly in excuse, 'He was only doing is best on my behalf.'

A sardonically sceptical brow ascended. 'I wouldn't like to see his worst, then, because his attitude sure leaves a lot to be desired!'

'Yes—well, he's not usually quite so— belligerent,' she felt obliged to defend. But not wishing to linger on the subject of personalities, she hurried to return the conversation to the matter that presently mattered most to her. 'And—and would your wife also be amenable to accepting Lief into her home?' When all was said and done, who knew better than she did just how unrelated persons could react to such situations?

Finch's mouth tilted crookedly. 'I don't happen to have a wife,' he advised in wryly drawling tones.

'Oh!' For some strange reason Blythe felt a warm flush mount her cheeks. 'Well, your parents, then?' She supposed they could own the homestead, in that case.

'They died some twenty years ago.'

'I see.' Her teeth began worrying at her lower lip. 'So you live on your own?'

'Well, in the house, anyway,' he allowed with a sudden, droll half-smile that to Blythe's disconcertion caused her pulse to leap unexpectedly, and left her feeling vaguely shaken. 'But as these two particularly family properties are run as a single venture, it's not often that there aren't relations of one kind or another around.'

Recovering, she nodded. 'It's just that normally when such guardianship and/or custody orders are made by the courts, they're in favour of married couples rather than single persons,' she explained anxiously.

'Although you have the boy, and you're not married,' he was quick to remind her.

'Because he's only in my care, not legal custody, at the moment. I was envisaging lodging a formal application once Nathan and I were married, but then . . .' She swallowed and pressed her lips together, reluctant to even think about Nathan's refusal any more. For the present she had to concern herself solely with Lief's welfare.

Finch's eyes became shadowed. 'No one else in

your family was interested in taking him in?' he queried in shortened tones.

Blythe shook her head. 'I don't have a family,' she disclosed regretfully, but grateful at least that he had refrained from making some acid retort concerning Nathan as a result of her unfinished comment—as she had suspected he might well have been tempted to do. 'Unfortunately, my parents are dead also, otherwise I wouldn't be here.'

Finch nodded slowly. 'Nevertheless, with regard to the legalities . . . it isn't unknown for single persons to be awarded custody in some circumstances, all the same,' he put forward in a thoughtful vein.

'N-o, I don't think it is,' she owned slowly. 'But living on your own, how *could* you take care of him properly? I mean, just while you're working on the property, there must be times when he wouldn't be able to be with you. And that's something the authorities would take into account too, I'm sure.' Her gaze turned worried once more.

'In which case, I guess I'll just have to devise some arrangement that will satisfy them,' he proposed with an unconcerned shrug. 'However, that's some way down the track as yet. In the mean time, I'm still waiting to hear just how you intend to ensure that—Lief, you say his name is?—will also be agreeable to living here.' He cast her a certain ironically expectant glance.

Blythe ran the tip of her tongue over her lips. 'I—well . . . I haven't really thought it over in—in detail,' she faltered. As she recalled, she hadn't been given much time to think about it at all, actually! 'I—I suppose I'll have to bring him up here one day, and—and then take it from there.'

A sound of disbelief issued from Finch's tanned throat. '*One* day for something of such importance? You're as incredibly magnanimous as your boy-friend is!'

'Well, what do *you* suggest, then?' she flared, stung. 'You're so damned smart, you tell me!'

'Gladly!' he had no compunction in firing back. Dragging his hat from his head, he raked a hand savagely through his dark hair, then clamped his headgear back into place more once. 'For God's sake, I would have thought it was obvious to anyone with even a modicum of intelligence—or compassion . . .'

'Don't you dare call me uncompassionate!' Blythe interjected wrathfully, her hands clenching tightly at her sides in an effort not to give in to the almost ungovernable desire to hit him.

'Although unintelligent is acceptable, presumably?' he promptly taunted, and had her temper bubbling even higher as a result. But before she could retaliate in any manner, he continued, 'And if you find it so objectionable, then I suggest you stop allowing all your thoughts and decisions to be dictated by what that petty tyrant over there might think or say!'

'I should let you dictate them instead, is that it?' she gibed tartly.

A slow smile suddenly spread across Finch's strong features, and his eyes grew lazy as they ranged over her upturned face in a lingering appraisal that had her swallowing convulsively. 'I suspect you would prefer the outcome if I did,' he contended in a soft drawl.

Even as she struggled to regain her equanimity —what was there about him that he should affect her so?—Blythe was still forced to concede that where Lief was concerned, at least, he was probably right. And since it was her nephew's welfare that was of paramount importance at the moment . . .

'All right,' she granted, if still not quite as composedly as she would have liked. 'So just what *do* you have in mind regarding Lief?'

Finch's expression became decisive. 'Initially, a visit, and in your company, of course, of at least a couple of weeks' duration, if not longer, in order to give him some chance to at least become used to his surroundings and his new family while in the presence of someone he knows.'

It seemed a reasonable enough proposition, Blythe supposed. Although it did present problems just the same. 'But I couldn't afford for us to stay at a hotel for that long,' she revealed doubtfully. And that would have been only if Yuroka's small hotel that she had glimpsed in passing did indeed provide such accommodation.

A sardonically dismissive curve took possession of his mouth. 'Besides being an arrangement that would hardly be likely to assist the child to settle in, anyway. For that to occur, the most logical and practical solution is for both of you to stay here on the property, of course.'

'W-with you?' The spontaneous words were out before Blythe could stop them, and she immediately flushed, berating herself for having openly displayed just what an unsettling influence his virile presence appeared to be coming to have on her.

'Well, I am Lief's potential guardian.' Finch fixed her with a wryly amused glance that only served to make her feel even more mortified.

She was twenty-two, and it had been some years since any male had managed to discompose her to such an extent.

'Yes—well . . .' She moistened her lips. 'None the less, surely it would raise a few eyebrows, and—and someone could even make some comment about it to Lief, if we—if we . . .'

'Just started living together?' he concluded for her with suspect helpfulness.

Blythe pressed her lips together and nodded jerkily. The connotation he had somehow managed to subtly infuse into the phrase had been impossible to overcome, or disregard.

'Well, don't let it worry you. I'm sure Verna—my aunt—and probably even Price too, if it comes to that, will be more than willing to move in with us for the time required in order to protect you from any nefarious designs I might have on your virtue,' he goaded, tapping her provokingly beneath the chin.

Blythe's face flamed with a combination of self-consciousness and vexation, the latter emotion fortunately enabling her to hold his chafing green gaze tenaciously.

'It wouldn't matter whether you did have any such designs or not, because I can assure you I'm quite capable of protecting myself in that regard!' she smouldered. 'My only concern was for propriety's sake—on Lief's behalf—nothing else! If he's going to live here, then I simply thought it in his best interest if his move could be achieved without creating any more gossip than his sudden arrival is likely to cause anyhow.'

'I see . . .' Finch nodded slowly, his lips twitching imperturbably. 'Then you have no fault to find with the arrangement on a personal basis?' He flicked her a watchful glance from beneath long sable lashes.

Did she now have any choice? 'I—I guess not,' she acceded grudgingly. 'Under the conditions you mentioned, of course.' The qualification was added as an afterthought, and in a considerably more challenging tone.

'Naturally.' There was an underlying facetiousness in his confirmation that had Blythe gritting her teeth irately. 'And your—boyfriend? Will he also have no objections?' drily.

Despite knowing it to be highly unlikely, Blythe adamantly refused to give ground and, accordingly, lifted her head fractionally higher. 'Well, even if he does, initially, I've no doubt he'll recognise the necessity for it in the end. After all, and as much as it may surprise you, it was Nathan who contended that we owed it to Lief's family to at least give them the opportunity to acknowledge and—and accept him.'

Finch promptly uttered a derisive laugh. 'Oh, that doesn't surprise me in the slightest!'

'Meaning?' She eyed him suspiciously.

'Just that, although there's been a considerable number of claims made this afternoon—by the pair of you, in fact—about acting in the best interests of others, one thing I do know . . . *He's* not considering anyone's interests other than his own!'

'And that's purely an assumption on your part!' Blythe defended swiftly. 'All right, so I admit his manner might have left something to be desired today, but he's not usually like that, and—and you don't know him as well as I do.'

Finch gazed at her askance, plainly unconvinced. 'Yeah, well, they say into every life a little rain must fall, don't they?' he mocked in a lazy drawl.

Blythe dragged in an infuriated breath. 'At least that's preferable to the positive deluge you're rapidly coming to represent in it!' she gibed. 'And I thought we were supposed to be discussing Lief . . . not Nathan!'

'That's fine by me,' he acquiesced smoothly. 'So when do you think you'll be arriving with the boy?'

Determinedly concentrating her thoughts, she did some mental calculations and put forward, 'Next Saturday . . . ?'

In response, and to her surprise, his eyes turned cool. 'You are in a hurry to—see him settled, aren't you?' A scornful brow arched high.

Blythe's lips compressed, but she did her utmost to control her again flaring vexation. 'In one way, yes, unfortunately,' she was forced to own heavily. 'Although not for the reason you evidently believe! Her voice rose challengingly with the urgent addition. 'It's just that he's due to start school for the first time next month, and since that can sometimes be a daunting experience, I thought it would be preferable if he wasn't also faced with the added burden of then having to change schools as well after only a short while.'

'Hmm . . .' Finch gazed at her measuringly for a few moments before finally nodding. 'OK, so next Saturday it is, then. What time do you expect you'll arrive?'

Blythe hunched a slender shoulder indeterminately. 'Much the same as today, I guess.'

'And you'll bring the relevant papers with you too?' His manner turned businesslike. 'A copy of his birth certificate, etcetera, and copies of his mother's birth and death certificates as well, I suppose. He'll no doubt need all that information later, even if I don't require it earlier when applying for custody.'

She swallowed painfully and nodded. The request had only served to remind her that she wouldn't be around to supply any of that information herself as Lief grew older.

'And you'll be staying . . . how long?'

Despairing over the knowledge that they could very well be the last weeks she would ever spend with her nephew, Blythe determinedly made the most of his prior recommendation. 'Two to three weeks,' she supplied on an almost defiant note.

Fleetingly, the hint of a wry curve touched Finch's lips, then disappeared again as he quizzed intently, 'You won't have any trouble in getting away from work for that length of time on such short notice?'

She shook her head decisively. The fact that the insurance company that employed her as a secretary intended closing its branch office in Geelong where she worked in six weeks' time had been a strong contributing factor in her decision to go along with Nathan's proposal that they come today. For in spite of the company's offer to find her another position in one of their Melbourne branches, the idea of either having to move to that city, or else travel an extra fifty miles to and from work each day—thereby leaving her even less time with Lief—she just hadn't been able to convince herself would be a satisfactory arrangement for either of them.

On the other hand, the thought of being out of work altogether, and still trying to support Lief while she sought another position in Geelong, had also caused her more than a few dispiriting, not to say panicking moments at the thought of what might happen if she did find herself unemployed for any length of time.

'No, I'm just about due for my annual four weeks' vacation, in any case, and as we're not particularly busy, anyway, at present . . .' She shrugged significantly.

'And your absence for that length of time will also be quite acceptable in *that* direction?' An explicit gaze was cast towards Nathan who was waiting, with clearly increasing impatience, beside their car.

Blythe's chin immediately elevated defensively. 'I don't see why not. He trusts me, and knows I wouldn't have agreed to it if there'd been any other option available,' she claimed, if with somewhat more outward than inward conviction.

Actually, she was sure Nathan would object to her absence for three weeks. The more so since it was to be spent in the company of the man to whom he had plainly taken such a dislike, and notwithstanding the fact that it would be to his own benefit in the finish. Not that any of that was Finch Carmody's concern, of course! she told herself resolutely.

'Then that would appear to settle the matter, at least for the time being,' Finch allowed, but to Blythe's ears, so drily that she couldn't help wondering with some chagrin if he hadn't been as aware of her thoughts as if she had voiced them. 'Except that I guess you'd better give me your address and phone number before you leave . . . just in case,' he went on in a return to his more pragmatic manner.

Nodding—it seemed a logical suggestion—Blythe began searching in her bag for a pen and some papers. But on being unable to locate any of the latter, she hesitated for a second or two before extracting the envelope containing the photographs of Lief and quickly note the requested details on that instead.

'You can keep the photos, if you want,' she offered in slightly husky tones as she held out the envelope towards him. 'I expect you'd probably like to see them again, and—and perhaps even show them to the rest of your relatives.'

Although Finch took hold of the small package, he didn't immediately relieve her of it, but remained with his fingers briefly overlapping hers. 'You don't want to keep them?' he hazarded quietly.

Blythe ran the tip of her tongue across her lips, suddenly unbalanced by the frisson of tension the warmth of his casual touch was generating. 'I—I can always get another set of prints taken from the negatives,' she stammered, and swiftly pulled her fingers free.

'Then thank you.' He inclined his head in appreciation. 'I'm sure everyone will be most interested in seeing them.'

'Yes—well . . .' Blythe brushed his gratitude aside with a shrug as she shifted uncomfortably from one foot to the other, abruptly anxious only to make her departure now. 'I—we'll see you on Saturday, then,' she said lamely, already beginning to turn away.

Finch nodded. 'I'll be waiting for you.'

Blythe merely responded with a faltering half-smile and started for the car on legs that seemed inexplicably unsteady. There was something about Finch Carmody—something indefinable—that warned she was going to have to be very wary in the weeks to come if she wanted to retain any peace of mind at all, she decided.

CHAPTER THREE

THE FOLLOWING week was a hectic one for Blythe.

To begin with, and exactly as she had anticipated, she had had to placate Nathan, whose feelings had become so ruffled at the mention of her impending three-week absence.

'Well, if that's the only way you think the matter can be settled once and for all, I guess I'll just have to go along with it,' he had eventually acquiesced, however, and to her relief, in his normally less belligerent fashion. Although that still hadn't prevented him from counselling, 'Just take care, that's all. I wouldn't put anything past that Carmody. He's too damned sure of himself by half!' A pause. 'And don't forget to keep in touch, hmm?' he had added with a rueful smile, and she had happily agreed.

After that, there had been the careful explanation to Lief that they had managed to locate his father's family, and that they had been invited to stay with them on their property near the mountains for a while. But whereas Nathan had taken the information amiss, Lief, she was thankful to note, accepted it with a quiet, but still unmistakable, sense of expectation that not even the painful advice regarding his father's death could entirely dispel.

51

The knowledge that he did actually have some family besides Blythe was evidently proving intriguing to him.

Then there had also been the business of arranging her release from work. An unaccountable feeling—or maybe just a subconscious wish to prolong her likely parting from Lief for as long as she could if it should become possible—made Blythe decide on the spur of the moment to hand in her notice instead of simply taking her holidays as she had originally intended. Her employment would only have lasted a further two weeks after her return, in any event, and as Nathan had commented, what did it matter when they would be marrying very shortly and his salary as a surveyor was more than sufficient to support them both very comfortably?

The remainder of her time had been spent in making last-minute repairs to some of Lief's clothes, packing all his belongings, her own clothes, booking her anything-but-new car in for a service and overall check in preparation for the journey, ensuring that the house was locked and secure while she was away, etcetera, so that by the time they actually came to leave on the Saturday she was grateful to at last have it all behind her.

'I like it when there's just the two of us, Blythe,' confided Lief shyly once they had been driving for a while. He had never called her aunt, due to Blythe herself having laughingly maintained originally that at seventeen she hadn't felt old enough to be so named. Besides, at the time she had thought of him more as a younger brother, in any case. 'You don't get angry when I ask lots of questions,' he went on to explain in a solemn voice.

Meaning, as Nathan did more often than not, she surmised with a sudden flash of resentment against her absent boyfriend. He made known his adherence to the old-fashioned belief that children should be seen and not heard quite repressively on occasion, she had to admit.

'Yes, well, Nathan just has an unfortunate way of speaking sometimes, I'm afraid,' she excused with a sympathetic smile, but not bothering to pretend ignorance all the same. 'So if you want to ask questions, from now on you just go ahead . . . OK?'

Lief nodded seriously, his small forehead puckering as he sought the right words. 'This uncle of mine—the one you told me about—is he nice?'

Finch Carmody—nice? Blythe's brows rose in wry speculation as she considered the matter, and found herself strangely unable, or unwilling, to categorise him with such a bland term.

'Well, you'll like him, I'm sure,' she temporised in lieu.

'But will he—like me?' Lief gazed up at her with suddenly doubtful eyes that had her heart constricting.

Oh, God, was this a result of Nathan's attitude towards him too? she despaired. Or was it simply a natural apprehension due to his never even having been aware of his father's family before, let alone met any of them? She could only hope the last was the reason.

'And why wouldn't he?' she countered, forcing a teasing smile on to her lips. 'You're not planning on suddenly turning into a little monster, are you?'

He gave a muted giggle. 'No, course not.'

'Then I've no doubt at all that he'll soon like you as much as I do.'

Seemingly satisfied with her answer, and with his attention distracted by the unfamiliar passing scenery, Lief soon had other queries to make, and during the remainder of their journey their sporadic conversation revolved around more general subjects.

However, when they reaced the Yuroka Valley and were driving along its length once more, it was Blythe's turn to feel apprehensive as they neared the end of the road. Lief, for the moment, showed only a childish eagerness at the thought of their staying on a farm, excitedly requesting to have the homestead pointed out to him immediately it came into view.

For Blythe, the moment held far greater significance, and she was abruptly unsure of everything. Uncertain whether she was doing the right thing by Lief, whether Finch was still of the same mind, whether she could bear to part with Lief if he was, whether Lief himself would ever be amenable to such a permanent change, and . . . yes, she finally had to admit, uncertain as to just how she was going to manage living in such close proximity to the strangely disruptive Finch Carmody!

In consequence, when they eventually drove over the cattle grid and up to the homestead, she stood nervously beside the car after alighting, leaving Lief to exclaim over, and attempt to make friends with on his own, the apparently ever-present welcoming committee of barking dogs.

The next instant an authoritative command in a deep male voice issuing from the veranda had the dogs promptly disappearing again, much to Lief's obvious disappointment, and looking in the direction of the house Blythe saw Finch descend the steps and move with a loose-limbed stride towards them.

Today he was clad in well-fitting fawn moleskins and a green-checked shirt, the rolled sleeves revealing his powerful forearms, his head of ebony-dark and lightly curling hair uncovered on this occasion. He also appeared relaxed, assured, and totally in command of himself and the situation —exactly the reverse of Blythe—and as a result did nothing to alleviate her own unsettled state.

'You're later than I expected,' he began conversationally as he passed through the gateway. Then, with his mouth tilting and a bantering look in his eyes as they ranged lazily over her, 'I was beginning to think you might have changed your mind.'

'N-o.' To Blythe's dismay her voice came out in a tremulous croak, and she swiftly indicated her vehicle with a deprecatory gesture in an effort to disguise her uneasiness. 'I—I'm afraid my car is somewhat slower than Nathan's, that's all.'

'I see.' He dipped his head wryly before turning his attention to his nephew, and Blythe waited with bated breath to discover just what their reaction to each other would be.

Sinking lithely down on to his haunches in order that their heads might at least be on almost the same level, Finch smiled easily into the small features that were regarding him with a certain wary solemnity. 'So you're Lief. I think I would have known you anywhere. You look a lot like your father, you know.'

'I do?' The response came on an almost breathless sigh of delight.

Finch nodded. 'Uh-huh! Very much so.'

'And—and you're my uncle that Blythe told me about?'

Briefly, an all too expressive green glance was slanted in Blythe's direction, as if mockingly challenging just what might have been said, and for a moment her heart skipped a beat for fear of him making some sardonic comment that might somehow rebound on Lief, but to her relief when he returned his gaze to his nephew, he merely nodded equably once more.

'Mmm, I'm your Uncle Finch. Although you can just call me Finch, if you like,' he invited, evidently picking up the omission of any such more formal title from his reference to Blythe. 'Your father was my younger brother.' He paused, inclining his head consideringly. 'Would you like me to tell you about him some time?'

'Oh, yes!' Lief's return was spontaneous, unequivocal, the look of sheer pleasure abruptly breaking over his face, and the intensity of his voice leaving no doubt in anyone's mind as to how he viewed the prospect.

And Blythe was shocked. Shocked to discover just how much Lief had apparently missed having a father; shocked and, yes, she conceded, disappointed with herself, to realise it hadn't even occurred to her that he might have felt that way; and even more shocked, not to mention discomfited, because it was clear Finch had somehow seemed to guess it, or at least suspect it, immediately.

With a shake of her head, she refocused her thoughts, and found Finch to be rising upright once more and suggesting to Lief, 'In the mean time, though, would you like to have a look around? See some of the animals, perhaps?'

Lief gave an eager nod, but still singled out, 'The dogs?'

Finch smiled. 'You like dogs, do you?'

'Mmm . . .' The small face fell a little. 'But I'm not allowed to have one at home. Blythe says our yard's not big enough, and a dog would get lonely on its own all day.' There was a heavy sigh. 'Nathan says they're a pest, anyway.'

Blythe promptly found herself on the receiving end of a pungent glance that said, 'Nathan would!' more plainly than if the words had been spoken.

'Well, I'll tell you what,' Finch began, returning his gaze to Lief. 'If you go up to that first shed there, you'll find half a dozen puppies inside with their mother. You pick one out, and you can have it as your own—for as long as, or whenever, you're here . . . OK?'

'Honestly . . . ?'

Finch smiled and nodded. 'Honestly.'

'Oh, thank you!'

Lief was rushing on his way almost before he had finished speaking and, watching him, Blythe was uncertain whether she was pleased because he seemed to have accepted Finch so quickly, or piqued because he hadn't sought her approval before hurrying to carry out his uncle's suggestion. He always did whenever Nathan made any recommendation to him.

With Lief's departure, Finch eyed Blythe's continuing position beside her car mockingly. 'You don't have to stand guard over it, you know. No one's going to steal it,' he drawled. 'Nor is anyone going to eat you, so there's no call for you stand there looking so wide-eyed and apprehensive either.'

Blythe promptly reddened, but was thankful that his goading remarks at least had the effect of finally snapping her out of the disconcerting, and vexing, state of nervousness that had beset her ever since entering the valley.

'And maybe I was just waiting to see when your aunt and uncle are going to appear!' she retorted. There had been no sign of them as yet, and surely they would have put in an appearance by now if they had been present. 'After all, their presence was a condition for our staying here.' She paused. 'Or don't you believe in keeping your word?' A partly accusing, partly gibing note entered her voice.

Finch tut-tutted chafingly. 'Them's fighting

words, sweetheart, so I'd be a little more careful in my use of them, if I were you,' he counselled lazily, and the bite that wasn't evident in his voice somehow gave Blythe more reason for pause than if it had been.

'Well, where are they, then?' she queried in a more moderate vein.

'For the moment, at home still. We didn't consider Lief's meeting the whole family, en masse as it were, would be anything but a little overpowering, and even confusing, for him, so Verna and Price will be over a little later.' His lips twitched. 'The rest of them will make his acquaintance during the following weeks.'

'The rest?' she hazarded doubtfully.

'Mmm, second and third cousins, etcetera, great-aunts and uncles, even a couple of great-great-aunts and uncles,' he elaborated in wry tones. 'The Carmodys have been in these parts for over a century now, and with the penchant they had in the past for families of upwards of a dozen kids, there aren't many people in the vicinity of a hundred miles round here that we're not related to in some way or other these days.'

Blythe assimilated the information thoughtfully. She hadn't realised just how accurate Nathan had been when, after checking the electoral rolls, he had declared that the whole area seemed peopled with nothing but Carmodys! she mused ruefully.

'In that case, I guess I actually owe you my thanks for not overwhelming him with relatives immediately,' she felt obliged to own, if abashedly.

And once having started, 'As well as for not disclosing that Lief's stay here could be a—permanent one, when you said about him having a dog of his own.'

Finch shook his head sharply in rejection. 'You don't have to thank me. It's not gratitude I want from you.' His expression assumed a sardonic cast. 'Or is it just that you think every male's as insensitive to everyone else's feelings but his own as your boyfriend is?'

Blythe gasped. 'That's not true! And you leave Nathan out of this!' She glared at him balefully.

'Then don't confuse me with him by assuming I'm any less capable than you are of deducing the effect news of that magnitude could have on the boy at this stage!'

Her breasts heaved. 'All right . . . I apologise for that, at least! Although I can assure you I wasn't confusing the two of you! How could I? I sincerely doubt you have a single characteristic in common!'

Abruptly, Finch smiled—a provoking moulding of his attractive mouth that promptly aroused a wayward stirring of her senses, but which simultaneously had her resenting the very magnetism that appealed to her.

'Well, that's a relief to know,' he quipped.

'As it doubtless is to him too!' Blythe sniped swiftly in return. 'But now . . .' With a supreme effort, she tamped down her flaring emotions resolutely in order to favour him with a sweetly mocking smile. 'If you have nothing more relevant to say, I thik I'll check on what Lief's up to, if you don't mind.' Finally making a move away from the car, she set off determinedly in the direction her nephew had taken.

'He's still deliberating over which pup to choose,' came the tongue-in-cheek, and totally unnecessary, advice from Finch as he easily kept pace with her. He slanted her a graphic sideways look. 'So tell me—what else does Nathan consider pests . . . besides children and dogs?'

Blythe's teeth clenched. *He does not consider children pests!* she gritted, keeping her eyes glued to the approaching shed.

'Just Lief, huh?'

'Not even him?'

'I suspect Lief might disagree with you on that point.'

She just couldn't let that pass, and coming to a sudden halt, she swung to face him fiercely. 'Oh, do you really! On the strength of a five-minute meeting you're an instant expert on his feelings now, are you?'

Finch's green eyes shaded ironically. 'I didn't even need five minutes to see just how wary and unsure of himself he was at meeting me.'

'Because he hasn't met all that many men, and he was afraid you might not like him, that's why!'

'And why in hell would that even occur to a child of his age . . . unless the only male he's apparently been in constant contact with had taught him to think that way?' His voice roughened with contempt.

Momentarily, Blythe stared at him indecisively. He couldn't possibly be right, could he? No, he couldn't be, she determined with a shake of her head. She would surely have realised it herself, and long before this, if there was any truth in his claim.

'That's pure supposition on your part,' she condemned as a result. 'Lief has always been somewhat on the quiet and—and withdrawn side. That's just his nature.'

'Or just another reflection of the environment he was raised in, perhaps?' Finch raised an explicit brow.

At the implied censure, Blythe's resentment flared. 'Oh, I see! So it's my fault as well now, is that what you're again implying?' she rounded on him bitterly. 'Well, when you've gone without as much as I have; when you've given up just about the whole of your social life; and when you've devoted as much of your time, effort, and care as I have to that child—and I don't regret a minute of it, because I'd willingly do the same again if I had to—then you can start casting aspersions on what I've done, Finch Carmody . . . but not before, do you hear?' She drew a shuddering breath. 'I've never claimed my efforts to have been perfect. I just did the best I could, that's all!' Anguished tears abruptly filled her eyes and she turned away quickly to hide them.

Then just as rapidly she was spun back to him, strong hands framing her face between them and forcing her to look up into the intense green eyes that were regarding her so closely. But when she reached up to drag his hands away, his words stopped her in mid-action.

'Don't you think I've already realised that?' Finch asserted gruffly in rueful exasperation. 'Don't you think I can guess how difficult it must have been for you?' He shook his head wryly. 'Stop being so defensive, for God's sake, will you? It's not you, personally, I'm critical of.' Smiling softly, he traced the outline of her imperceptibly quivering lower lip slowly with his thumb. 'It's more—those around you.'

Blythe trembled, unbelievably conscious of his unexpected action, of the hands still cupping her face, the feel of his sun-warmed skin beneath her own fingers as they remained curled about his strong wrists.

'*Those* . . . around me?' she queried shakily in some confusion, dropping her hands quickly to her sides now.

Finch hunched a muscular shoulder. 'Well, apart from the most obvious one . . . you said yourself, Lief's mother was indifferent to him. So between the pair of them, I wouldn't have said there was much reason for him to ever be particularly —exuberant.' He paused, then added drily, 'Besides, he looks so much like Danny that I can't quite bring myself to believe that's all he inherited from his father, because Danny could never have been said to possess a retiring nature and, if nothing else, he openly enjoyed every aspect of life to the fullest.'

'If not always carefully,' Blythe felt entitled to remind him pointedly.

'In this instance, it would appear not.' Finch

inclined his head in acknowledgement. 'Although had he been aware of the result of his meeting with your sister, he wouldn't have evaded, or ignored, the consequences of his actions, I do know. That wasn't Danny's way.' Removing his hands from her face at last, he trailed a finger evocatively along her jaw. 'As I've said before, the Carmodys have always believed in taking care of their own.'

Blythe swallowed and nodded weakly, and was glad of the interruption when Lief's excited voice abruptly broke the silence, diverting Finch's attention, and allowing her to rally her scattered defences as she watched her nephew's hurried approach.

'Look, Blythe, look! Isn't he beautiful?' Lief exclaimed, referring to the squirming, blue-speckled pup clutched in his arms. The pup licked at his ear enthusiastically, making him gurgle with pleasure. 'I'm going to call him Benjie.' Then, with his expression turning a little anxious as he gazed up at Finch, 'Or has he already got a name?'

Finch shook his head. 'No, not as yet. Although I feel I should point out that your he is a she, and therefore another name might be little more appropriate.' He spared Blythe a humorous glance that had her responding helplessly.

'Oh!' A frown descended on to Lief's forehead and for a moment he looked stumped for words. 'I know . . . I'll call her Pixie, then,' he declared at length, his face clearing once more. 'Is that all right?'

Finch nodded. 'In fact, you can help name the

rest of the litter as well, if you like.'

'Oh, yes!' The suggestion found favour with Lief immediately. 'Now?'

'Well, maybe not right now,' intervened Blythe with a smile. 'Why not save that for another day? You have the other animals to see yet, remember?'

Lief nodded happily, no sign of his earlier apprehension visible at all now as, by common consent, they began heading past the sheds to the horse paddock beyond.

CHAPTER FOUR

BLYTHE awoke slowly the following morning and, judging that it was still reasonably early by the quietness and the light filtering through the lace curtains at her bedroom window, made no move to rise immediately, but lay musing drowsily over the events of the previous afternoon and evening.

That Lief was already close to hero-worshipping Finch there was no doubt, she reflected. And why not? the wry thought promptly ensued. The easy manner in which his uncle related to him, the patience he displayed when explanations were required, and the way he instinctively seemed to know what would appeal to and interest Lief, were a powerful combination to resist. And resistance, of course, was the last thing on Lief's mind.

Unlike her own, she paused to insert somewhat self-mockingly. But since the unnerving effect Finch appeared to have on her at times wasn't a subject she cared to dwell on for too long—just what was it about him that could suddenly make her emotions churn so unexpectedly?—she swiftly, and determinedly, channelled her thoughts back to her nephew.

Initially, on meeting Verna and Price

Carmody, Finch's aunt and uncle, Lief had become a little withdrawn again, although Blythe had taken to them immediately. Both grey-haired and in their middle fifties, they were a comfortable, down-to-earth couple. Verna, plump and motherly, but with a ready laugh and smile that was warming and would prevent her from ever appearing old; her husband much taller and even more solidly built, his face craggy and lined, though still far from unhandsome, and possessed of a pair of lively hazel eyes that denoted an astute intelligence and good humour.

Already with four children of their own, it transpired they had also willingly added Finch and his brother to that number when they had lost their parents in a light plane crash, and the way in which they had obviously drawn their nephews into their home and lives had relieved Blythe of any fear that they wouldn't also soon have Lief at ease with them too.

Exactly as had shortly proved to be the case, for by merely treating him as just another member of their own family they had gradually won his confidence, so that by the time Price began regaling him after dinner with some of Finch and Danny's boyhood deeds, it was becoming clear he was beginning to settle in with a speed Blythe would never have believed possible.

But now, as she stretched languidly, Blythe's attention was distracted by the sound of muted voices, punctuated by a feminine laugh, coming from the rear of the house, and abruptly realising that it wasn't *that* early for Lief not to have come seeking her by now, she threw back the covers and slid her feet hurriedly to the floor. She didn't want Verna thinking she expected her to look after Lief entirely during her visit. Come to that, nor did she *want* to relinquish her care of him completely either.

Presently, her toilette hastily concluded, and dressed in pale blue denims and a sleeveless cotton top, Blythe made her way quickly to the kitchen, the source of the voices she had heard. Although not before first checking on Lief's room where she indeed found his bed deserted and the clothes he had worn the day before also missing. Nevertheless, when she entered the kitchen, only Verna and Price were in evidence, partaking of a cup of tea from the large pot resting amid the other breakfast impedimenta atop the obviously already utilised check cloth-covered wooden table.

'I'm sorry I'm late. You should have woken me,' she began apologetically. Then, with a frown, 'But have you seen Lief? He wasn't in his room when I looked.'

'No, he's with Finch and the boys, so there's no call for you to worry. They'll see he comes to no harm,' Verna set her mind at rest with a reassuring smile as she set about pouring Blythe a cup of tea. 'You just come and sit down, and have your breakfast in peace. There's bacon and eggs, sausages, steak and chops, whatever you prefer.' She rose to her feet in order to start her preparations.

'Oh—er—whatever's easiest. I don't want to put

you to any trouble,' Blythe replied self-consciously, taking a seat at the table. Her expression took a rueful turn. 'I'm obviously going to have to rise earlier in future.' And that despite the clock on the wall showing it was still only seven-thirty!

'But it's no trouble,' she was assured earnestly while Verna set about putting some rashers of bacon in a pan. 'And of course you don't have to rise earlier. We realise you're probably not used to the hours we keep in the country.'

'Besides, we figured you were more than likely tired after your drive yesterday,' put in Price.

Blythe hunched a deprecatory shoulder. 'Yes, well, that's very kind of you, but I still wasn't expecting to be waited on while I was here.' She wanted to make that clear at least.

'But you're our guest!' Verna sounded genuinely shocked at the idea that Blythe might consider it otherwise. 'It's the least we can do in return for your bringing Danny's son to us.' She paused, a reminiscent smile catching at her mouth. 'He's so like him, and he is such an appealing child, isn't he?'

A sentiment Blythe could never dispute. 'Yes, very much so,' she agreed sincerely, even as mention of Lief recalled to mind a previous remark. 'But you said—he was with Finch and . . . the boys?' Her brows lifted quizzically.

'Mmm, Jarred and Nicol, our two eldest,' Price enlightened her as his wife busied herself adding eggs to the bacon. He gave a wry chuckle. 'Not that I suspect that either of them, at twenty-nine and

twenty-seven   respectively,   consider
themselves—boys.'

'No, I suppose not.' Blythe laughed with him.
'Although it's thoughtful of them to have
apparently taken the trouble to come over to meet
Lief. He'd appreciate that.' She released a sighing
breath. 'It wasn't really until yesterday that I
actually realised just how much he's evidently
missed having a father and—and an extended
family. I guess he must have heard the other
children at kindergarten talking about theirs, and
felt—left out.' She bit at her lip regretfully.

'But not because of any omission on your part in
view of what Finch has told us,' Verna hastened to
impress on her encouragingly. 'And certainly Finch
and the boys,' with an expressive glance at her
husband, 'will ensure he never feels that way again.
You can rest assured they'll always do the right
thing by Danny's son. It's only a pity we didn't
learn of his existence sooner.' She hesitated, and
then added gently, 'We would be interested to learn
something of his mother, though.'

Blythe licked her lips and nodded. And for the
next half hour or so, while she ate, she did her best
to give a résumé of her sister that was fair in
delineating her good points as well as the not quite
so good ones. After all, Petra hadn't ever been
deliberately unkind to Lief, she defended to herself.
She had simply preferred to leave it to others to
take care of him—in much the same way, Blythe
supposed, as did those people who hired nannies to
look after their children.

Then from outside abruptly came the sound of galloping hoofs, coupled with a childish treble of laughter, and followed shortly by running footsteps crossing the veranda.

'Blythe, Blythe . . . come and have a look!' Lief burst out excitedly, erupting into the room, his hair tousled, his cheeks glowing. 'Finch caught a—a brumby in the mountains last week which he says I can have all for my very own once he's bro-broken in! And he says he's going to take me in to town tomorrow to buy me some moleskins just like his, and some stock boots too, for me to wear when I learn to ride!' Catching hold of her hand, he began tugging at it urgently. 'Oh, do come and look at him!'

'Finch?' She half-smiled teasingly.

Momentarily, he stopped pulling and stared at her blankly. Then he uttered a giggle and shook his head. 'No, my horse, silly!' Succeeding in finally propelling her to her feet, he went on, 'Oh, he is nice, Blythe. He's black with a white . . . star?' he looked to Price for confirmation of the description; continuing after receiving a smiling nod in response, 'on his forehead. And that's what I'm going to call him too . . . Star,' he announced proudly.

'Well, that would certainly sound appropriate,' Blythe allowed. 'But . . . a brumby?' She glanced at Verna and Price a trifle worriedly. Was a former wild horse really the most suitable for a child, and particularly one who had never ridden before?

'Oh, there's no worry. They really make excellent stock and packhorses, as well as children's mounts,' Price was quick to assure her. 'Having roamed the mountains all their lives, they're very steady on their feet, especially in rough country, and if put to work up there mustering, they also have the added advantage of possessing an unerring instinct for finding their own way and picking the best routes to follow.'

'I see,' she acknowledged on a relieved note, glad to have had her fears laid to rest.

'So now will you come and look at him?' put in Lief, gazing up at her pleadingly.

Blythe hesitated, not wanting to disappoint him, yet simultaneously feeling obliged to point out, 'Well, I really should help your Aunt Verna,' as Lief called her, although strictly she was his great-aunt, 'to clear and wash up the breakfast things first.'

However, Verna herself wouldn't hear of that, and determinedly bustled them both from the kitchen, claiming her husband would be more than able, and happy, to provide any assistance that might be required.

They found Finch and his two cousins—Lief surprising Blythe by taking it upon himself to perform the necessary introductions with unaccustomed aplomb—leaning negligently against the waist-high fence that surrounded the homestead as they awaited Lief's return, a couple of saddled horses cropping desultorily nearby, and she was immediately struck by the amazing similarity of all three men.

Except for the slightly different shape of his mouth and teeth, Jarred could almost have been Finch's twin, she decided. While Nicol, an inch or so shorter than the other two, and stockier, his features only minimally different, possessed the identical hazel-green eyes that Lief had turned on her so imploringly such a short time ago.

As a result, when she and Finch set off on foot to view Lief's mount—Jarred and Nicol being prevailed upon by Lief to ride down in order that he might be taken up in front of one of them, as they had apparently been doing beforehand—her curiosity got the better of her and she turned to him quizzically.

'Verna and Price's other two children . . . they also look much the same as the rest of you, do they?' she enquired wryly.

Finch noddded, his mouth shaping humorously. 'Except that Brent's hair is more brown than black, and Nerida's eyes are a definite brown.' His gaze turned bantering. 'I did tell you last week that a certain similarity of appearance wasn't uncommon among the Carmodys around here.'

So he had, she mused ruefully, but refused to allow him to distract or unsettle her. 'They didn't come with Jarred and Nicol to meet Lief, though?' she queried.

'Couldn't,' Finch supplied casually. 'They're up on the high plains this weekend,' he nodded towards the high and rugged mountains that rolled majestically away into the distance beyond the valley, their sunlit peaks and ridges etched clearly against the azure skyline, 'spreading salt for the cattle we graze up there during the summer.'

'Spreading salt?' Her brows lifted questioningly.

'Mmm, on the rocks so the cattle can lick it off. Although the variety of feed up there is very good for them, the ground's deficient in salt which they need to stay healthy, so we usually take some up every couple of weeks.'

Blythe frowned. 'Isn't that a nuisance?'

Finch laughed, his white teeth contrasting strikingly with the deep bronze of his tanned face. 'Not when the mountains are in your blood; when there's nothing quite like the feeling of riding those high plains and valleys, no matter what the reason; and when its grandeur and its challenges have been a part of your life—as with your father's, grandfather's, and great-grandfather's before you—for almost as long as you can remember.'

Blythe's eyes widened. She hadn't anticipated such depth of feeling. 'And is that also why you take your cattle up there in summer?'

'Uh-uh!' Finch shook his head. 'It's because they do so well up there, and not only with regard to condition either. They don't suffer from internal parasites as they can do in the paddock, and they're stronger through the exercise they get walking up and down the hills, so that come calving time the cows, and even the heifers, usually give birth with far greater ease that might otherwise be the case. It also allows us to carry a heavier stocking rate because it means the farm paddocks aren't being eaten out, which in turn permits us to cut more grass for hay to feed them during winter.'

Blythe nodded. 'Although you apparently still don't take all your cattle up there,' she remarked curiously, noting the, admittedly few, red and white-coated animals visible in the paddock beyond the holding yards they were approaching.

'No, we usually only take our best cattle because, as the land up there is leased from the government, they stipulate the numbers allowed . . . on ours, as well as all the other similar such leases. We're not the only cattlemen to take our stock to the high plains each summer, of course.'

'No, I had realised that,' Blythe returned thoughtfully. Who hadn't either seen on TV, or at least heard of the annual cattle drive when all the high-country cattlemen took their stock up into the mountains to graze—and the week-long general muster that preceded them bringing the cattle down off the ranges prior to the first major snowfall of winter.

'What do you think of him, Blythe? Isn't he great?' Lief's excited voice now had her redirecting her thoughts as they reached the yard containing his horse, and she smiled to see him clambering up the rails in order to obtain a better view.

'Yes, he's very nice,' she lauded dutifully, even as she eyed the distinctly nervous and snorting animal somewhat askance. 'And you're very lucky to have a horse of your own, but . . .' she glanced round at the three men—Jarred and Nicol still mounted, but each with a long leg thrown casually over the pommel of his saddle; Finch with his forearms resting on the top rail as he surveyed the yard—to query of them collectively, dubiously, 'are you sure he's an appropriate mount for a child?'

'I wouldn't have suggested it if I didn't think so,' came Finch's expressively drawled contribution.

'Sure, once he's broken in, he'll be a different animal,' predicted Nicol.

'And with a bit of stock work first to settle him right down, he'll be as steady as you could want,' Jarred concluded with a nonchalant confidence that was undeniably comforting.

'It won't take too long, though, before he's broken in, will it?' Lief put in anxiously, and once again surprising Blythe with his eagerness. Riding wasn't an activity she would ever have imagined him anticipating with such enthusiasm. 'There will be time for me to ride him before we have to go back home to Geelong?'

For a brief second no one spoke, and then Finch reached out to rough his hair companionably. 'You can be assured of that,' he told him decisively, and Lief's worried look was immediately replaced by one of relief.

'Meanwhile, however, we . . . ,' Jarred inclined his head to indicate his brother, 'still have a fence to mend this morning,' he advised on a rueful note, placing both feet in the stirrups once more.

Doing likewise, Nicol added enquiringly, 'You coming to give us a hand, mate?'

Initially, Blythe assumed he was addressing Finch, until she saw him extend an arm towards Lief.

'Oh, can I?' It was almost possible to see her nephew's small chest puff with pride at being addressed in such an egalitarian fashion. 'Can I, Blythe?' He gazed at her hopefully.

She spread her hands in a helpless expression. 'I guess go—if Jarred and Nicol are willing . . . and you're back in time for lunch.'

'We'll see he is,' promised Nicol, edging his mount closer to the rails and, catching hold of Lief about the waist with one arm, he swung him easily into position in front of him.

'And you'll really let me help?' Lief twisted around to ask.

'Of course.' It was Jarred who answered. 'With that extra assistance we'll probably finish in half the time.'

Lief smiled blissfully, and then innocently proceeded to disclose, 'Nathan never lets me help him do anything. He always says kids my age are . . .' he frowned in concentration, 'more trouble than they're worth.'

For the second time in almost as many minutes there was an abrupt silence, and Blythe felt the hot colour of mortification dyeing her cheeks. From the discomfited looks on Jarred and Nicol's faces, she didn't doubt they were well aware who Nathan was—and just how their cousin regarded him. While as for Finch himself—well, she simply refused to even glance briefly in his direction, knowing already precisely what his expression would be. The only one unaware of the impact of his words was the person who had uttered them, and her eyes lifted to her nephew's despairingly.

'Lief!' she gasped at length on a slightly strangled note. 'I've never heard him say anything of the kind!'

'But he has said it, Blythe, lots of times . . . honest!' he insisted earnestly. 'Maybe you just weren't there when he did.'

Blythe caught at her lip with even white teeth. Lief was neither a liar, nor in the habit of making up stories, she knew, and yet . . .

'Well, whatever, we don't happen to think that way. We'll be glad of your help,' Jarred interposed with a smile. Then raising a hand to his cousin and Blythe, 'We'll see you later.' He wheeled his horse towards the head of the valley.

'Yeah, we'd better be off,' agreed Nicol in somewhat relieved tones, and set after his brother at a canter with one arm firmly wrapped about the small figure before him to keep him in place.

'Faster, faster!' Lief's laughed urging floated back to the yards, but Blythe already had other things on her mind as she braced herself for the comments she just knew Finch was going to make.

Although when they did come, she was thrown off balance a little by them taking a totally different form from that anticipated.

'And you're still intending to marry someone with an outlook like that towards children,' Finch began by mocking reprovingly.

Blythe dropped her gaze, moving from one foot to the other. 'Since it's not the—um—impression I've received . . . yes,' she pushed out in a voice that was far weaker than she would have liked. 'He—he would be—different—with his own children, anyway.'

'Would he?' A sceptically arching brow made his opinion plain.

'Well, of course he would,' she maintained a little more firmly. 'Isn't everybody?'

'Will you be?' subtly.

'That has nothing to do with it,' she alleged, albeit somewhat blusteringly. 'In any case, you know nothing about what Nathan's really like.'

Pushing his hands into the back pockets of his moleskins, Finch leant negligently against the yard rails. 'So why don't you tell me, then?' he invited lazily.

Blythe eyed him askance. 'Because I doubt you're really interested,' she half sniped, half snapped.

Finch hunched a broad shoulder idly. 'Try me.'

Blythe pressed her lips together, unsure whether he was amusing himself at her and Nathan's expense or not. Then, deciding she owed it to Nathan at least to put the record straight, she returned his gaze defiantly.

'All right. Where I'm concerned, he's usually considerate and—and amenable. He definitely isn't purposely goading, or mocking, that's for certain!' she inserted with pointed pungency. 'He's also calm and composed, and comfortable to be with.'

Briefly, silence reigned, as if he was waiting for her to continue, but when she didn't, his brows arched chafingly. 'And you're satisfied with that?' he probed on a drawling note of disbelief.

Blythe drew a nettled breath. 'I can't think of any reason why I shouldn't be!' she flared.

'With calm, composed, and comfortable?' Finch repeated sardonically, easing himself away from the rails. 'Shouldn't there also be at least some excitement, some fire, some passion there somewhere? Or is he just so impassive, or indifferent, that he's never tempted to do this?' He swept her against his hard form unexpectedly, his mouth determinedly taking possession of hers.

Stunned by the suddenness of his action, Blythe momentarily offered no resistance. She was only aware of the persuasive demands of his mouth as it moved on hers, expertly, sensuously, and she gasped as she felt a surprising warmth beginning to spread through her body.

Now she did start to fight against him, in something of a panic—this couldn't, shouldn't, be happening!—and yet, even as she attempted to drag herself free, she knew her lips to be waywardly parting, responding, to the seductive pressure his were exerting. And as his seeking tongue entwined erotically with hers, left no part of her warm mouth unexplored, her struggles gradually diminished and finally ceased.

Suddenly she seemed to have no will of her own, merely an incomprehensible desire to surrender to the unruly feelings he was arousing so skilfully, and to her disconcertion she found herself melting pliantly, against him her arms wrapping about him of their own accord, her hands clinging tightly to the ridged muscles of his broad back.

With a sound of satisfaction, Finch ran his hands down her curving form slowly, possessively, pressing her even closer to his muscular length, and making her pulsebeat quicken as she realised the extent of his own arousal. The fact that it should have been Nathan's kisses she was returning so uninhibitedly, his caresses turning her blood to liquid fire, her body appeared to have resolutely, unaccountably, renounced; her dazed and reeling mind seemingly incapable of combating the ardent assault that was stimulating feelings she had no business experiencing.

Then his fingers were brushing her nape, weaving within the bright strands of her hair, his lips grazing the soft skin beneath her ear, tracing a leisurely path to the exposed and throbbing hollow of her throat before reclaiming her mouth once more, and his tongue resumed its probing, luring, intimate invasion with a hunger that had her trembling uncontrollably.

His own breathing unsteady, Finch at last raised his head to gaze down into her flushed and bemused features, his green eyes dark and still smouldering with lingering emotion.

'He must be an even greater fool than I thought, if he doesn't make love to you,' he murmured on a huskily rough note.

So shocked was she by her own behaviour, it took Blythe a while to realise he was referring to Nathan, but when she did, it only served to magnify the enormity of her lapse of fidelity, and proportionately increase her embarrassment as a result. The more so since she suspected mockery had been the guiding factor behind both Finch's actions and words.

'While I would have thought Lief was the perfect example why self-control should be practised!' she retorted, seeking alleviation of her own discomposure in anger. Her accompanying effort to gain freedom proved more successful than her previous attempts had been—although doubtless only because he had been prepared to release her this time, she grudgingly had to concede. 'And you had no right to—to kiss me like that,' she continued to censure, albeit with a self-conscious falter. 'Nathan is the only one with any—rights in that regard . . .'

'Even though, judging by your response, he apparently doesn't avail himself of them?' Finch broke in to quiz in a taunting drawl.

'That's not true! And—and you caught me by surprise, that's all,' she asserted, even as she reddened ungovernably.

A lazy smile made an appearance. 'I'll keep that in mind for next time.'

Blythe sucked in a sharp breath. 'Except that there isn't going to be a next time!'

Finch shrugged imperturbably. 'We'll see.'

'No, *you'll* see!' she contradicted with a sardonic nod for emphasis, and took to her heels before he could reply—or was tempted to put her claim to the test. Something she strongly suspected he was more than capable of not only attempting, but to her trepidation, quite possibly accomplishing.

CHAPTER FIVE

'WELL, Lief seems to be taking to the life here most enthusiastically,' Nerida Carmody commented to her family in general one evening some two weeks later after Lif had departed the sitting-room in order to fetch his puppy so that he could demonstrate to her how the dog's training was progressing.

With their parents having changed residence temporarily, it had gradually become the habit for all four of Price and Verna's children to join them for the evening meal, at least, these days. Although in this instance, it was Nerida's first visit for a couple of days—she having dined with her fiancé, Russ Haddon, a member of the district's other most prolific and long-established cattle-raising family, on those occasions—and consequently was the reason for Lief's eagerness to show off his pup's progress now.

The dark-eyed girl promptly followed her remark with a slyly bantering glance cast in Finch's direction. 'Which, of course, means there's all the more reason for you to marry Delvene, doesn't it?' she proposed. 'After all, at Lief's age, he really needs a mother too.' She paused before adding significantly, 'As I was only saying to Delvene just last night.'

'Were you now?' Finch returned her gaze wryly.

Nerida moved forward on her chair, warming to the subject. 'Well, you must admit she's perfect for you. And I'm not just saying that because she's my best friend, or because she's Russ's sister, either.' The qualifying insertion was voiced swiftly. 'I mean, I know you like her, and you've been out together quite a number of times. While as for Delvene . . .' her mouth curved whimsically, 'well, as we're all aware, she's never shown an interest in anyone but you ever since high school. What's more, our two families have always been close; she's aware what running a property entails; she's good at handling the stock; she's an excellent cook; she's pretty and practical; and importantly . . . she likes Lief.' She shrugged and spread her hands meaningfully. 'As I said, she's perfect for you.'

What Finch said in reply, or even if he did contribute to the remarks that ensued, Blythe didn't hear as she became lost in her own thoughts on the matter.

She had met Delvene Haddon, and her brother Russ, on a couple of occasions now, but despite having privately considered the other girl a little too demure and perhaps even submissive, at the same time she couldn't deny that Delvene had seemed to sincerely take to Lief, and would undoubtedly be a good mother to him. She now also supposed that it must have been marriage to Delvene that Finch had had in mind when he'd claimed that, if the courts made it necessary, he would solve the problem with an arrangement that was satisfactory to them.

However, the thought of their possible, and undeniably suitable marriage promptly seemed to engender an odd feeling of depression. Although more than likely only because it meant Lief would be out of her own care completely then, Blythe rationalised swiftly. Besides, it wasn't as if moments of dejection were anything new to her of late, anyway . . . and for almost the same reason. In fact, as the days had inexorably passed, and Lief spent more and more of his time in the company of the Carmodys rather than herself, those moments had become increasingly frequent.

It wasn't that she begrudged him any of the time he spent with his new-found relatives, or their time with him. It was just that her own last weeks with him were flying past all too rapidly, and with nowhere near the amount of contact between them to make it any easier. She had said originally that she would be staying for two to three weeks, but most of that had disappeared already, and although she knew she couldn't expect to extend her visit indefinitely, she still hadn't been quite able to bring herself to the point of actually sounding out Lief's feelings with regard to remaining permanently. As she had divulged to Nathan the last time she phoned him, she recalled with a sigh.

'Well, it's probably for the best. The main thing is that the boy's apparently more than content with his father's relations,' had been his reply, but which somehow seemed to have missed *her* point, and consequently left her no less reconciled.

Now, as Lief returned to call Nerida from the room, Blythe felt the prick of involuntary tears as the two of them disappeared together, knowing that once it would have been to herself that her nephew would have been so proud and keen to display his dog's prowess. So when Verna said she would make some more coffee, it was Blythe who hastily volunteered to do it in her stead, and made for the kitchen before she embarrassed herself, and everyone else, by being found crying over what had really been such a trivial occurrence.

She had only just refilled and switched on the drip-percolator when she heard a step behind her, and then her face was tilted up to the light by a hard hand suddenly cupping her chin.

'I thought as much,' Finch declared on a deep note as he surveyed her still misty eyes and damp lashes. He shook his head regretfully and touched the back of his fingers to her cheek in an strangely comforting gesture. 'You feel you're losing him, don't you?'

His preception surprised her, as did the fact that he should have been the one to notice the cause of her hasty exit from the sitting-room. 'Something like that,' she confessed throatily.

'Although it's never been our intention to take him away from you, you know. You'll always be welcome here.' He paused, his mouth quirking briefly. 'Though preferably without your—lesser half, of course.'

Blythe bent her head. She doubted Nathan would ever want to come, anyway. 'Thank you,' she just managed to get out past the lump in her throat. 'I—I know you haven't deliberately set out to—to make me redundant, and really, for Lief's sake, I'm pleased that he's accepted you all so well . . . even though it may not look like it at the moment.' She tried to make a joke of it, but her voice quavered ignominiously and she turned away, her eyes starting to water traitorously again. 'It's just that—it's just that . . .' She shook her head helplessly, unable to continue while striving so desperately to check the tears that were spilling on to her lashes once more.

Then all at once she found herself being held reassuringly against a hard chest and a soothing hand stroking her hair.

'It's just that, unfortunately, that doesn't make *your* loss any the less painful, hmm?' Finch deduced heavily.

Blythe could only give a weak nod, surprised by her willingness to remain exactly where she was, and wondering why Nathan, who knew her so much better, hadn't also been able to grasp how she felt. Nathan also disliked tears, considering them a sign of a lack of fortitude, she recollected, and yet Finch, who was unquestionably more blatantly virile both in person and attitude, was apparently the more understanding of the two.

'So have you actually mentioned anything to Lief yet about him remaining here?' he asked in gentle tones.

'No, n-not so far,' she replied unsteadily, tearfully. 'I'm afraid I just haven't been able to bring myself to—to say anything about it yet.' The admission came on a broken note.

Finch's arms tightened about her imperceptibly, and her body seemed to welcome the closer contact, seeking strength from his nearness. 'Would you prefer it if I did it instead?' he offered.

It was a tempting thought, but one she reluctantly had to decline all the same. 'No, it's—my responsibility, and I think I owe it to him to be the one to tell him,' she put forward tremulously.

'You're sure?'

She sighed and nodded.

'You know you can always extend your visit, if that would make it any easier.'

Just as she had contemplated earlier? Blythe shook her head. 'Thank you all the same, but unfortunately, I suspect it wouldn't,' she lamented, struggling hard to regain at least some control. 'I'm sure we both know—what his reaction is going to be. While as—as for me . . . well, continuing to put off the fateful moment will only prolong the agony, I guess.'

Once again her face was tipped up to his. 'Nevertheless, let me know if you do find you want some help, after all, eh?' Bending his head, Finch unexpectedly brushed his lips fleetingly against hers.

It was the first time he had made any such move since that day at the yards, but despite the briefness of the contact and the lack of intensity, Blythe still found the impact of it on her emotions no less perturbing, not to say unsettling.

'Yes—well . . . I—I'll keep it in mind,' she stammered distractedly, and as much as the arms about her had previously proved to be reassuring—maybe even too much so, she acknowledged agitatedly—she now pushed free of them hastily. 'And I apologise for having given way to tears so easily,' she continued, self-consciously averting her gaze. 'I don't normally, and I'm sure you have better things to do than—than consoling an over-emotional female.'

'Better . . . than kissing you?' Finch was humorously incredulous. The lazy look he gave her was filled with an awareness that had Blythe colouring helplessly and vainly attempting to defend herself against the disturbing feeling of vulnerability that assailed her.

'Except that I—that you . . .' She broke off discomfitedly, unsure just what she did want to say. Then her gaze chanced to alight on the now full coffee jug and she gratefully grasped the opportunity it afforded. 'Anyway, the others must be starting to wonder what's happened to their coffee by now,' she claimed in a rush. Switching off the percolator, she picked up the jug and was already on her way to the door before enquiring over her shoulder, 'Are you coming?'

'I'm right with you, sweetheart,' drawled Finch, and she swallowed, unable to refrain from wondering if there hadn't been some double meaning contained in his words.

Not that Blythe allowed the matter to remain in

her mind for long, regardless. When all was said and done, she did have more perturbing questions to answer, she reflected anxiously. The most disconcerting one being . . . since she was going to marry Nathan, why should Finch have such a troubling effect on her?

During the next couple of days, as she tried to prepare herself mentally to broach the subject of his future with Lief, Blythe found herself watching her nephew even more closely, and noting the unanticipated changes in his behaviour that she couldn't help but admit were occurring.

She could well remember asserting to Nathan that Lief had never had any great penchant for outdoor activities, although to see him now as he took to his riding lessons with such enthusiasm, and eagerly participated in every farm activity available, she ruefully began to wonder how she could ever have made such a statement. Not only that, but he appeared to be definitely more confident in himself and outgoing too, and even in those few short weeks she could have sworn he had grown some as well.

Of course, that not the least of the reasons for the changes in Lief was the Carmodys themselves, and the easy and warm-hearted manner in which they had welcomed him so sincerely into their family, she couldn't deny. It was obvious his father, Danny, had been very popular, both within his family and the community in general. As were the rest of the family also, it had soon become evident. And why not? They were a very engaging lot, Blythe had to concede.

Nevertheless, the fact that the changes in Lief were so great and so noticeable only succeeded in engendering escalating periods of distressing self-doubt on Blythe's part. Was it possible that Lief's true nature had really been repressed all these years without her realising it? She hated to think that might have been the case, even if his present demeanour did confirm her move in bringing him here as being the right one, and it did at least provide the incentive for her to finally grasp the nettle the following afternoon as they sat together looking over the valley and raise with him the matter of his remaining with Finch.

'You mean, stay here for always? Not go back to Geelong?' Lief questioned immediately she hesitantly mentioned the subject, his eyes lighting up at the thought.

Blythe nodded, concealing the desolation the idea generated.

'Oh, yes!' His response was unqualified, and so was the pleasure evident in his expression until he hazarded warily, 'Nathan too?'

Blythe pressed her lips together, vexed with the absent man for causing such a reaction. 'No, not Nathan. He'll be staying in Geelong,' she advised as steadily as possible. Pausing, she inhaled deeply before going on to query in tentative tones, 'And would you still prefer to stay if—if I couldn't be here as well?'

He stared at her uncomprehendingly. 'But why

couldn't you? You like it here, don't you?'

Blythe sighed and nodded. 'Unfortunately, though, it's not quite that simple, love, I'm afraid. You see . . . the Carmodys aren't my family, so I don't belong here like you do.'

'But I'm still—*your* family, aren't I?' Lief turned worried eyes up to hers in confusion.

Blythe hugged him to her reassuringly. 'Of course you are! And you always will be! It—it's just that I'm going to—marry Nathan, and—and . . .' she swallowed painfully, 'Finch would like you to remain here when that happens.'

'But not without you, Blythe!' he protested in shaky tones. 'Why don't you just marry Finch instead?'

Blythe flushed in spite of the innocence of the suggestion. Solutions were always so simple to children, if not always feasible. 'Because I—love Nathan,' she attempted to explain.

She felt his small body tremble. 'And you like him b-better than me?'

'Oh, no!' she denied vehemently, her eyes closing momentarily in despair. How could she explain that there were different kinds of love? How could she expect him to understand the differences? 'Don't ever think that, Lief! It's because I love you so much that I think you should stay here . . . where I know you'll be happier. And you do prefer it here, don't you? You like being with Finch—and Jarred and Nicol, and everyone—better than with—Nathan?'

He nodded slowly, if a trifle jerkily, his face

suddenly taking on the solemn expression she knew of old. Only this time, to her astonishment, she saw in that instant a startling resemblance to Finch reflected in the unyielding set of his youthful jaw as he rose to his feet. It seemed that his time with the Carmodys hadn't only converted him to their way of life, but he was beginning to manifest family characteristics as well, Blythe realised in surprise.

'But I still only want to stay if you do too, Blythe,' he said quietly, and in such a self-contained fashion that it only served to remind her of his uncle once again. 'Only if you do!' he repeated on a rising note, and, his composure abruptly breaking, he went running towards the shed where Finch was working on some machinery.

Although Blythe immediately gained her own feet, intending to follow him—she couldn't leave him in such an obviously distressed state—no sooner had she taken a few steps than she came to a halt again, her teeth worrying at her lower lip.

Perhaps, as Finch had proposed, she did need some help after all, she brooded. Since it was to him that Lief had evidently gone, maybe he could succeed where she had failed. She doubted he could do worse—perhaps she should merely have let Lief become used to the idea of staying, before mentioning her own departure?—and there was always the possibility that, with his arguments added to hers, Finch just might be able to persuade him to accept her leaving. Lief usually hung on his every word these days, and she could only hope they might influence him on this occasion as well.

In fact, when next she did see Lief, an hour or so later, it seemed Finch might indeed have been successful, for all the earlier signs of agitation had disappeared from her nephew's demeanour as he excitedly took Nerida, who had just arrived with two of her brothers, to view the litter of kittens that one of the farm cats had given birth to only that morning.

However, as anxious as Blythe was to learn from Finch just what had been said, Nicol and Brent's presence deterred her. She thought the matter best discussed privately. As a result, and to her frustration, it wasn't until his cousins departed for their own home quite late in the evening, and Verna and Price began preparing for bed, that an opportunity at last presented itself.

'Could you spare me a moment, please . . . to talk?' she asked hurriedly when Finch also made a move to leave the sitting room.

Having already risen to his feet, he now lowered his length on to the padded arm of the sofa instead, leaning back negligently and giving a indolent inclination of his head. 'Any time, sweetheart,' he averred in a lazy drawl. 'So what's on your mind?'

Blythe averted her gaze briefly, wishing inconsequentially that when she had his undivided attention, as now, she could accept it with indifference rather than the unruly and unnerving awareness that immediately swept over her. For that and other indefinable reasons, he made her more flustered than she cared to admit, even to herself.

'I—I spoke to Lief this afternoon . . . about him remaining here,' she stammered in consequence. Then, glancing at him apprehensively from beneath her long lashes, 'Although he's already told you that, I suspect.'

'Uh-huh! We had quite an enlightening talk about it.' His lips twitched. 'He can display a surprising tenacity on occasion.'

As if she didn't know exactly where that trait came from! 'And . . . ?' she prompted apprehensively.

A watchful look filtered into Finch's green eyes. 'You know he thinks of you as his mother, don't you?'

That was part of the problem. Moistening her lips, Blythe nodded.

'So what do you intend doing about it?'

She frowned, perplexed. What did he expect her to do? 'Try harder to convince him it's in his best interests to stay here, I suppose,' she proposed with a sigh.

Finch's mouth shaped ironically. 'He's well aware of that already. He's more than willing to stay.' He paused, his ebony-framed eyes holding hers steadily. 'The question now is . . . are you?'

Blythe stared at him as if transfixed. 'M-meaning?' she just managed to get out faintly.

'To make a proper family unit it requires a mother as well, and since the courts do look more favourably upon married couples in custody cases, I obviously need a wife too,' he relayed matter-of-factly.

Blythe shook her head in disbelief. 'You're suggesting we . . . m-marry?' she stuttered incredulously.

Finch smiled wryly. 'That's the general idea.'

'But—but Delvene . . .' She said the first thing that came to mind, and then gasped in horror on realising that it should have been Nathan's name to have sprung immediately to her lips. Whatever could have possessed her? It must have been solely due to the unexpectedness of the suggestion, she excused guiltily.

For his part, Finch merely hunched a dismissive shoulder. 'It's not Delvene Lief wants here. It's you.'

Mention of her nephew brought a sudden recollection to mind. 'And was this also his idea?' she hazarded on a taut note.

'Lief's?' There was nothing feigned in the look of surprise that crossed Finch's face, or the amused laugh that followed. 'Why on earth would you think that?' He slanted her a lazily bantering glance that left her feeling short of breath. 'Or don't you think I'm capable of choosing for myself who to marry?'

Blythe coloured hotly and waved a distracted hand. 'Of—of course.' And feeling obliged to explain, however reluctantly, 'It—it's just that he suggested—something similar this afternoon,' she added.

'Then at least two of us would appear to be in agreement.'

Blythe sucked in a lungful of air and sprang agitatedly to her feet. 'There's more to it than that, Finch.' She began pacing about the room, unbelieving that he could be proposing such an idea so calmly, so—so idly. While her mind was reeling, he seemed completely in control, sure of himself, at ease, amused even, as he leant casually against the back of the sofa with an almost languid grace, his sinewed arms folded across his broad chest, his emerald eyes watching her lazily. He exuded an air of overwhelming confidence, his presence dominating the room to such an extent that it suddenly felt too small, and increased her own disconcertion as a result. Swallowing, she continued flusteredly, 'I mean, there—there's Nathan to consider, for a start. It was only because of our intended marriage that I brought Lief here in the first place.'

'But since you were also the one to have made yourself indispensable to the boy, can you really now deny that bond altogether and turn your back on him simply for your own—convenience?' Finch countered on a subtle note.

'That's not fair!' she immediately protested resentfully. He was merely attempting to make her feel guilty, and God knows she felt regretful enough already! 'I might also point out that you were quite in agreement with the arrangement until now!'

'Well, with Lief remaining here, at least,' he acceded cryptically, and she stared at him askance.

Just what was that supposed to imply? Somehow she didn't think she wanted to know and, half turning away, she touched a fingertip absently to the petals of one of the roses in the vase on the fireplace mantel.

'In any event, I want—children of my own,' she declared in defensively defiant tones.

'So do I.'

Blythe's breath caught in her throat, her heart starting to pound with erractic strokes as she swung back to face him involuntarily. So he wasn't even intending it to be a platonic relationship, she realised shakily, and couldn't understand why in heaven's name she didn't simply veto the whole idea once and for all by delivering a definite refusal.

Yet, inexplicably, the words wouldn't come. Instead, to her dismay, she suddenly found herself wondering just what it would be like to share the intimacies of married life with Finch Carmody; to experience again the sensuous demands of his mouth on hers as she had that day at the yards; to have her smooth skin caressed by those strong, capable hands that could control a fractious horse with such ease, and yet still frame her own face so gently; to feel his hard, muscular body pressed close to hers without the restrictive barrier of clothes between them, and to know the possessive invasion of . . .

With a gulp she gave a clearing shake of her head to dismiss the disturbingly intrusive images, if not the ungovernable flush that washed into her cheeks at her thoughts. Lord, she must be missing Nathan's caresses—no matter how circumspect or controlled—more than she realised!

'But—but we only met less than a month ago,' she burst out distractedly. 'You know nothing about me. Nor I you.' The amendment was hurriedly added.

A whimsical curve caught at Finch's mouth. 'Although I should imagine marriage would undoubtedly rectify that in very short order,' he countered with a droll inflection, and her colour deepened at the connotations his words evoked. 'And I'm prepared to take the chance for Lief's sake.'

Which, Blythe supposed, was very generous of him considering the length of time he had known his nephew. But more to the point, would a marriage based on such a reason, and on such short acquaintance, even have a chance of succeeding? Then, of course, just how could she explain such a decision to Nathan?

The thought had her gasping abruptly. Oh, God, she was actually considering the suggestion, she recognised, aghast. Marriage to a high plains cattleman, at that! One of a close-knit and select group whom she had not only never expected to meet, but whose way of life was completely foreign to her. Oh, why couldn't Nathan have been more like Finch in his attitude towards Lief?

But he wasn't, she had no recourse but to acknowledge in frustration, whereas Lief *was* her only living relative, was a part of her fun-loving sister and, by no means least, was the person who had come to mean so much to her. Could she really turn her back on all that . . . even for Nathan? She had thought she could, provided Lief settled in well to his new life, but now . . .

'You don't think marriage is a somewhat extreme solution to the problem, when my departure was only mentioned to Lief for the first time this afternoon?' she demurred as a last resort. 'I mean, once he's had time to become used to the idea, the matter may be able to be resolved in a less—less drastic manner.'

Finch quirked an ironic brow. 'If by that you mean he's likely to change his mind regarding you staying, then going by his reaction today, I suspect you're underrating the depth of his feelings for you . . . and the extent of his determination,' he declared drily.

Or at least the determination you appear to have imbued him with! amended Blythe inwardly with a grimace. Nevertheless, the relentless and shaming thought ensued, if he was prepared to give up Delvene for Lief, could she, caring for her nephew and his happiness as she did, now in all conscience do any less? It appeared not.

'All right, I agree,' she assented crisply at last, striving resolutely for the same matter-of-factness with which he had originally put forward the suggestion. 'When do you propose the marriage should take place?'

To her surprise, and some confusion, Finch displayed no emotion—satisfaction, relief, or otherwise—at her decision, but merely inclined his head smoothly in acknowledgement.

'In view of the arrangements that will need to be made, I guess four or five weeks would be appropriate,' he advised. 'Provided you consider that sufficient time in which to finalise your own affairs, of course.'

Blythe frowned. 'But I thought those were the arrangements you were referring to.' After all, she had to break the news to Nathan, and his reaction wasn't going to be either resigned or brief! she just knew. Then there was the house to either arrange to have rented or sold, various government departments to be contacted regarding Lief, plus a host of other matters that would require attention. 'Apart from applying for a marriage licence, what other arrangements are there to be made here?' she questioned dubiously. She presumed they would be married in Yuroka since there seemed no point in him travelling to Geelong for the ceremony when they would be living in the valley.

At that, Finch did show some emotion, his mouth crooking with rueful humour as he leisurely eased himself upright from the sofa. 'When a Carmody in this district marries, you'd better believe it requires a great deal of arranging. Because they are never private nor insignificant affairs, I can assure you,' he relayed explicitly.

Blythe shook her head in rebuttal. 'But I was envisaging something small and—and low-key. I mean, it's not as if this marriage is anything like a normal one.'

'Isn't it?' He began moving towards her and she watched his approach with suddenly widening and wary, darkening grey eyes.

'I—well—the marriage isn't for normal reasons, then.' She forced a deprecatory shrug.

'*Our* marriage . . . not the, or this marriage,' Finch corrected in sardonic tones. Catching hold of her wrist, he lifted her hand to his mouth, his lips pressing against her palm before capturing her fingers one by one, his tongue caressing the sensitive pads with a slow, deliberate sensuousness that made her every nerve-ending quiver and sent an aching sensation down her spine. 'Or are you just afraid to admit that our living together may prove you're not as unresponsive to your physical needs as you apparently like to imagine?'

Momentarily, Blythe struggled for breath and a return of reason. She didn't know whether it was because of his action, or because she was so conscious of their continuing nearness, but she was suddenly very aware of how easy it would be for him to take possession of her mouth in the same unsettling fashion he had her fingers.

Then, in a desperate effort to concentrate on something other than the way his lips would feel against hers, she agitatedly pulled free of his grasp and whirled away to a safer distance. She couldn't trust her turbulent emotions, and when she eventually spoke she only just remembered to keep her words and manner as impassive as possible, in line with her earlier decision.

'I'm sorry, but you seem to be labouring under some misapprehension,' she declared, standing her tallest and hoping her voice sounded more dispassionate than she felt. 'I'm neither afraid, nor have I any reason to imagine anything. I'm simply finding it difficult to reconcile myself to marrying anyone but Nathan, that's all.' She mentioned the other man's name purposely. 'So now—if you'll excuse me, it's getting late, and I have a lot to think about . . .' She began hurriedly making for the doorway.

'Don't forget to include . . . how *un*satisfying you would have found marriage to him, will you?' Finch promptly drawled mockingly behind her, but although she stiffened, Blythe didn't stop or turn back.

Oh, hell, just what had she got herself into? she despaired once she was safely inside her room. She must be mad! Marriage wasn't something to enter into on the spur of the moment—even for the sake of a beloved nephew—and especially not with a man who turned her emotions upside down with such disconcerting ease. Marriage should be a commitment to love, as it would have been with Nathan, and yet . . . And yet the minute Finch touched her, he aroused feelings Nathan never had, she couldn't help but recall with some bewilderment—and disquiet.

CHAPTER SIX

THEY WERE married a month later in the small
and pretty red brick church in Yuroka. The
absence of any relatives on Blythe's side, apart
from Lief, was more than compensated for by the
number of Carmodys plus associated relations
and acquaintances present.

Price did the honours in giving Blythe away;
Nerida was her only attendant, not only due to
the time factor, but also because of Blythe's
insistence that the wedding was merely one of
convenience. For the same reason, she had
declined to be married in a traditional bridal
gown, selecting instead something much more
simply styled.

Even so, as the service progressed, Blythe
found it impossible to remain entirely unaffected
by the occasion. It *was* a momentous event, and
no matter how hard she tried to remind herself
that it should have been Nathan standing next to
her, from the time Finch had taken her hand in
his she had felt her senses waywardly succumbing to the hallowed atmosphere of the flower-
filled church, the evocative ritual, and not least
an overwhelming consciousness of her husband-
to-be.

Did he have to look quite so handsome, so vibrantly masculine, so decidedly captivating? she thought irrelevantly. In contrast to Finch's easy, assured demeanour, she was a mass of nerves and apprehensions, and never more so than when it came time for their vows to be sealed with the customary kiss. The disturbing effect of it was completely out of proportion to the gentle pressure exerted and the length of time their lips met.

Then shortly they were emerging on to the church steps to face cameras, showers of confetti, and a colourful, cheerful throng all eager to offer their congratulations and good wishes. Blythe was thankful for the opportunity provided to recover her composure, and was warmed by the kindly and good-hearted manner in which she was welcomed into the Carmody family.

She knew there were two, though, who didn't view the marriage happily—Nerida and Delvene. The latter, understandably, since she had never made any attempt to disguise her feelings for Finch; although her behaviour was beyond reproach, nevertheless, as she bravely proffered her sincere felicitations, she unknowingly made Blythe feel even more discomfited as a result.

Nerida, on the other hand, had made her objection known openly and immediately on first learning of the proposed marriage. And not only because she had wanted to see her best friend married to Finch, but also because she had made it clear she considered he deserved better than to marry solely in order that Blythe might remain with Lief. In fact, Blythe suspected, it had only been due to her mother's prevailing upon her that Nerida had agreed to act as her attendant—she being the only female in the immediate family of much the same age—although when it had actually come to the day, it seemed it had become a case of the family closing ranks, for there had been no sign of any opposition in either her expression or manner as Nerida fulfilled her duties faultlessly and with seeming willingness.

The reception was held at Price and Verna's home, or more precisely in the gardens surrounding the homestead, there being just too many guests to be accommodated inside, despite the larger than normal size of the house. The catering was a family effort—as was normal on such occasions, Blythe discovered—with all the Carmody females providing an assortment of dishes, and usually those for which they were justly renowned, so that the burden of preparing the food never fell to only one person. Of necessity, the liquid refreshment was also a variety, catering as it had to for both adults and the large number of children present, and as the sounds of conversation and laughter began to flow freely, Blythe sipped absently at her own sparkling champagne, her thoughts turning involuntarily to Nathan.

To say he had been incredulous on hearing of her intention to marry Finch, when she had returned to Geelong to attend to her affairs, would have been to minimise his reaction, she reflected. Absolutely flabbergasted would have been more like it, and it had been some days before he would actually accept that she really meant to go through with it. Then he had shown moments of anger, affront, acrimony, and even vexed disbelief on being unable to change her mind.

Her only defence had been that he was more able to deal with her desertion than Lief would have been, but although he had taken strong exception to her reasoning, she had noted disappointedly that it still hadn't been to such an extent as to have him altering his own decision where her nephew was concerned. Consequently, he'd had no option but to eventually resign himself to the inevitable, even if he evidently wasn't in compliance with it.

'Cheer up, this is supposed to be a wedding, not a funeral!' her reverie was suddenly disrupted by Finch chiding in a drily drawled undertone as he refilled her glass.

Pressing her lips together, Blythe gave him back a look as provoking as his own. 'I was just thinking about Nathan,' she disclosed with bittersweet deliberation.

Finch bent his head mockingly. 'Then I guess your downcast expression was perfectly understandable. Thoughts of him would be sufficient to desolate anyone.'

'Except that wasn't what I was meaning!' she gritted.

He uttered a softly reproving, goading sound. 'Then you're either purposely blind, or a masochist, not to have realised what life with him would have been like.'

Blythe's grey eyes flashed indignantly, and she took a mouthful of her champagne in an attempt to cool her temper. 'While I'm more inclined to think I'm a blind masochist for having agreed to marry you!'

Catching hold of her free hand, Finch lifted it to his mouth, his lips brushing slowly across her knuckles. 'Then I guess I shall just have to convince you otherwise, shan't I?' he murmured subtly, and the nerves in Blythe's stomach tightened.

'As long as you remember I only agreed to the arrangement for—for Lief's sake,' she stammered uneasily, snatching her hand away.

'What else?' he countered with an indolent smile, raising an innocent brow.

Blythe flusteredly averted her gaze, suspecting he was playing cat and mouse with her, but unwilling to say or do anything that might prove her right, or conversely, put ideas into his head that perhaps weren't already there regarding the exact state of their relationship.

In view of the fact that no further mention had been made in that direction since Finch had first voiced it, she was more than content to leave it that way. She was already too confused and perturbed by the traitorous response he drew from her senses at times, and she still felt conscience-stricken for having so faithlessly forgotten Nathan each time it happened. After all, Nathan was the man she was supposed to be in love with!

By now, however, Finch's attention had been diverted and held by someone else, Blythe was grateful to find on eventually returning her gaze in his direction. It enabled her to relax to some extent, although as night inexorably replaced day, the younger children were put to bed in the house, and as the evening gradually wore on, she was aware of an increasing tension inside.

Despite being thankful no one had suggested a honeymoon—apart from the most obvious reason, summer was also a very busy time on the property—Blythe still found it impossible to view her approaching wedding night, and all the nights thereafter, with anything like equanimity. Just what was Finch expecting of her?

There had been no mention of them sharing a room, let alone a bed, but at the same time she couldn't entirely forget his previous declaration about wanting children of his own either . . . or the fact that, for tonight at least, they would have the house to themselves. It had already been decided that Lief would stay the remainder of the night with Verna and Price in their home to save waking him.

Consequently, when Finch eventually remarked that he thought it was time for them to leave, Blythe could only nod limply, and hope that her outward appearance didn't reflect the nervousness that made her feel as taut as a drawn crossbow inside when they finally made their departure amid much geniality, and drove the short distance back to Finch's house.

'Well, I trust your wedding day wasn't too unenjoyable for you, Mrs Carmody,' he remarked on a wryly bantering note as they alighted and headed for the homestead.

Her new title sounded strange to her ears and threw Blythe even further off balance. 'Oh—er—everyone was very kind and welcoming, thank you,' she pushed out jerkily.

'Then just to complete it, I guess this is in order too,' Finch drawled, and before she could divine his intent, he had scooped her into his arms to carry her effortlessly up the steps and across the veranda.

Totally distracted by the feel of his muscular form so close to hers, the strength of the corded arms about her, Blythe promptly squirmed agitatedly in an effort to be set free.

'Oh, please! There's really no need for this,' she protested in somewhat breathless tones.

Not that her plea had much effect, for Finch merely manoeuvred them so that he could open the front door and then carried her inside where, still without releasing her, he switched on the hall light . . . and his lips shaped obliquely as he leisurely scanned her wide-eyed and apprehensive features.

'I know the tradition of carrying the bride over the threshold is supposedly in memory of the Romans' abduction of the Sabine women, but if you're going to continue looking as if you're expecting to be ravished, maybe I should fulfil my part and do just that. After all . . .' his voice deepened, and he bent his head to stroke her ear with his tongue, 'as the saying goes: "If you've got the name . . ." '

Blythe quivered, her heart suddenly thumping with a thick, heavy beat. His face was so near she could discern every detail: the firm, well-shaped mouth; the lean and determined jaw; the startling green of his eyes within their thick, dusky lashes; and she was abruptly assailed by the disquieting suspicion that it wasn't mere awareness that flustered her so whenever he touched her, but shockingly, a subconscious wish to respond.

'Ex-except that *I'm* not interested in—in anything of the kind, Finch!' she burst out frantically. 'The more so with the memory of Nathan so fresh in my mind.' Once again she introduced the other man's name purposely, but this time she knew immediately that she had miscalculated badly as she saw the considering glint that entered his narrowing eyes, and his mouth curving into an ominous line that presaged no good for herself.

'So Nathan's memory is still fresh in your mind, is it?' Finch mused in a dangerously silky voice as he at last set her feet to the ground. Although not in order to release her, but simply to entrap her struggling form against him more securely. 'Or should that be . . . imaginings?' His voice became laced with mockery. 'Because

Nathan was always too composed, too controlled—or too cold!—to create any memories of substance by actually making love to you, by showing you the pleasures a man's touch can really bring, wasn't he? I'll bet Nathan's never done this . . .' He pushed aside the loosely draped neckline of her dress to explore a satin-skinned shoulder with his mouth. 'Or this . . .' His voice roughened as his lips scorched a trail to the rising swell of her full breasts, sending a warm shock through her that slowly splintered her nerves. 'Or this . . .' His mouth closed possessively over hers, sucking her lower lip between his own, and tracing the velvety surface inside sensuously with his tongue.

Blythe trembled, mortified by the way in which her senses had responded at the first burning touch of his mouth. No, Nathan hadn't ever done any of those things, hadn't ever made her so aware of her own needs, she acknowledged shakenly, but . . . Oh, God, what kind of a woman was she, that the caresses of a man she didn't love could arouse such tempestuous feelings? The perturbing thought provided the impetus for her to drag free of the continuing assault of Finch's mouth that was slowly but surely eroding her will to resist.

'Finch!' she protested as firmly as she was able. 'This has gone far enough.'

'The hell it has,' he denied thickly, his eyes smouldering with an intensity that gave evidence of his own arousal. 'It's time you learnt there's a whole lot more between a man and a woman than the half-hearted experiences you've obviously been used to.'

Her words of dissent were cut off before they had even begun as his lips returned to plunder her mouth with a knowing, invading, seductive skill that further alarmed her. Her mind seemed to be waging a futile fight with her body. One wanting to repudiate him and the drugging emotions he was relentlessly stirring; the other mutinously intent on succumbing.

And in the end her body won. On a sighing breath she subsided against him helplessly, her arms clasping about his broad back, her lips clinging to his unreservedly and matching his sensuality with an abandonment that had his breathing deepening. Blythe tasted of him now, and Finch moulded her to his muscular form more tightly, kissing her with a ravaging hunger that sent currents of fire lapping through her blood and an aching sensation downwards to her thighs.

She could feel the entire length of his body, hard and demanding, pressed against her, his hips moving urgently against her own, and her hands dug deeply into the dark thickness of his hair as she was shaken by the tumult of emotions that overwhelmed her.

Finch uttered a sound low in his throat, and keeping her close with one hand, cupped a rounded breast with the other, his thumb massaging the nipple to a swollen peak that

surged against the delicate silk covering it. Wild
sensations immediately racked Blythe's whole
being, and she couldn't control the gasped
murmur that escaped her, or the violent tremor
that followed.

Certainly Nathan's restrained embraces had
never prepared her for the feelings that were
swamping her now, or the fervent wanting that
Finch's fiery touch engendered. Never in
Nathan's arms had she felt this burgeoning
excitement that made her body tingle and her
heart pound.

But when, for the second time that evening,
Finch abruptly gathered her into his arms and
carried her swiftly into his bedroom,
reality—shocking, sobering—suddenly intruded,
and her hands splayed across his chest, forming a
frail barrier between them, as he set her down on
the wide bed.

'Finch . . . no!' She tried to make it an order,
but the dryness of her throat made it more of a
husky whisper. 'I'm not interested in—in making
any . . . comparisons.'

Cradling her face between his hands, Finch
smoothed a thumb slowly across her lower lip,
making her even more vibrantly aware of him; of
the warm masculine feel of him, the sense of
vigour and strength that aroused the femininity
in her as no one ever had before.

'Your body says differently,' he contradicted in
throaty tones.

Blythe flicked her tongue over her lips, unconsciously following the path his thumb had taken. 'I—I've probably had too much champagne,' she excused herself with a frantic breathlessness.

Despite her efforts to keep them apart, Finch eased her fractionally closer, his hands dropping to her shoulders as he bent to set his mouth to the exposed line of her jaw, his tongue sensuously stroking the vulnerable skin.

'And *in vino veritas*,' he countered. 'Isn't that how the saying goes?' His hands moved around her smoothly to the zipper at her back and deftly slid the fastener downwards.

Blythe stiffened. 'No . . . don't!' The protest was made in alarm as the soft material promptly slipped from her shoulders and the draped neckline sank embarrassingly low. Clutching at the fabric, she strained away from him agitatedly. 'Or—or doesn't it occur to you that I might just have been substituting you for Nathan?' she threw at him wildly on a panicking note.

Finch shook his head and drew her nearer, imprisoning her hands between them. 'Except that it was *my* name you gasped so feverishly just a few short moments ago,' he revealed resonantly, his expression gently mocking, and she flushed helplessly at the recollection.

At the time she hadn't known what she had said, but obviously he had heard.

'And you'll do the same again before this night's through,' Finch continued in the same deep vein, the prediction somehow no less shocking to Blythe than the feel of his fingers suddenly easing beneath the loosened material of her dress and, swiftly freeing the taut fullness of her breast from her bra, close about the firm flesh possessively before she could prevent it.

In spite of the denial that rose to her lips, it was never voiced as spasms of raw pleasure shot through Blythe at the exploring caress of his hand. Then, suddenly, Finch was impatiently edging her dress still lower, baring her swelling breast to his darkened, lingering gaze. Blythe uttered a soft moan, but whether in satisfaction or belated objection even she wasn't certain. She knew she should object, make at least some form of protest, but her brain wouldn't seem to function properly. Not while she ached for him to continue. Instead, she arched towards him, her fingers digging convulsively into his shoulders to draw him even closer, and at last surrendering completely to the fiery sensations he was evoking.

Reluctantly releasing her breast, Finch lifted his head, his breathing as heavy and uneven as hers when their gazes locked, and she shivered at the naked desire visible in his eyes. Grazing the curve of her throat with his hands, he wove his fingers into the silky strands of her hair.

'No, my beautiful, stubborn wife, it's not Nathan you want, it's me . . . and just as much as I want you,' he murmured rawly, his mouth finding hers as he bore her back against the soft pillows at the head of the bed.

With her lips immediately parting beneath the sensuous demands of his, Blythe didn't answer.

In fact, she was beyond words. She was only aware of the feel and taste of him, the hard muscularity of his powerful form, and the shocking acknowledgement that he was right. She did want him, and as she had never wanted Nathan. She wanted his touch, wanted his possession, and abruptly, fiercely, she wanted nothing between them; only the virile heat of his naked flesh pressed against the pliant softness of her own.

Slipping her hands inside his shirt, she trailed them savouringly over his wide chest, curling the whorls of hair round her fingers experimentally before sliding her arms around him to caress the hard muscles of his back.

'I want to feel your skin on mine,' Blythe suddenly found herself owning against Finch's drugging mouth, and in a voice so hoarse with passion that she hardly recognised it as her own, much less believed she had actually made known her desire so blatantly.

'God, so do I!' Finch groaned, already shrugging out of his jacket as he rolled lithely to his feet.

In the faint light from the hallway, he stripped swiftly. His skin was warmly bronzed, his stomach flat and hard, his body as impressively sculptured as she had imagined it to be—and unmistakably taut now with evident need. Within seconds he was beside her again, his hands moving surely to remove the frustrating encumbrance of her clothes before pulling her back into his arms with a sound of undisguised pleasure as flesh met willing flesh.

Feelings she had only half dreamed coursed through her veins and she moved feverishly against him. Her fingers dug into the muscles of his back, kneading the taut flesh convulsively. She felt as if her skin was on fire. No matter where he touched her with his mouth or hands, fiery needles of pleasure pierced her, and instinctively her fingers began to travel hungrily over his muscular body too. They glided across the width of his shoulders, caressed the length of his spine and lean flanks, and she revelled in the feel of his muscles tightening sharply beneath her questing fingertips, in the knowledge that she could arouse him as satisfyingly as he did her.

And when the release finally came, it took them together to rapturous heights, wave after wave of exquisite pleasure washing over Blythe in an eruption of sensation that had her involuntarily crying aloud with the ecstasy of it.

On her eventual return to reality, it was to find herself being cradled gently in Finch's arms, his hand smoothing her tousled hair from her forehead, and replete with a sense of utter well-being, Blythe allowed him to mould her still sweat-moist body unresistingly to his muscular frame.

He felt warm and comforting and pleasantly protective, and for the moment she was quite content to leave it that way. Nevertheless, as her eyelids gradually became heavier and she began to drift into sleep, she suspected drowsily that it was entirely possible she might come to think otherwise in the cold light of day.

Blythe came awake slowly the following morning, stirring languidly, and uncomprehending of the strange weight that seemed to lie across her legs.

'Good morning. How did you sleep?'

At the unexpected sound of Finch's indolent enquiry, her eyes flew open rapidly, all trace of delicious lethargy abruptly leaving her as she instantly recalled the happenings of the previous night, and promptly despaired at the memory. God! What on earth had possessed her? Immediately, she shied away from that provoking question, her face burning ungovernably, and attempted to concentrate on the present.

'I—er—slept very well, thank you,' she replied primly, suddenly realising that it was one of his legs thrown over hers that was creating the feeling of weight, and hastily making an effort to extricate her own from beneath it. In vain, as it turned out. 'And—and you?' she appended, more to keep her mind off their embarrassingly naked proximity than because she had any desire to know.

Finch's mouth tilted into a lazy smile and he trailed a finger along the exposed line of her shoulder, making her swallow nervously. 'With your warm and curving shape in my arms, how could it have been anything but satisfying?' he murmured.

'Yes—well . . .' Blythe moistened her lips, and struggled into a sitting position—only just managing to keep herself covered with the sheet. 'I—um—think it's time I was getting up now, so . . .'

'What's your hurry?' he interposed protestingly and, looping an arm about her waist, he effortlessly made a mockery of her attempts to put more distance between them by drawing her back to his side again. 'It's still early yet.' He paused, his hand sliding upwards to cup a full breast. 'And after last night I can think of nothing more I would rather do than . . .'

'Well, I can!' Blythe broke in on him frantically, thrusting his hand away, and abandoning all thought of working around gradually to expressing her feelings on the matter.

Inescapable fingers closed about her shoulder when she would have begun moving away again. 'And what's that supposed to mean?' Finch demanded, his green eyes narrowing as he propped himself up swiftly on one arm, leaning towards her.

Swallowing, she moved restively. 'I'm sorry, but last night was a—a mistake.'

'Not as far as I'm concerned, it wasn't.' His mouth shaped expressively. 'Nor you either at the time . . . going by your response.'

Blythe crimsoned. 'W-well, now I can see that it was, and—and I regret . . .'

'Having demonstrated that you do actually

have desires and needs only a man can satisfy, and more particularly that your emotionless Nathan never did fulfil?' The query was inserted roughly. 'For having wanted me just as much as I wanted you?'

She bent her head, but still persisted resolutely, 'Yes! I regret all of it!' Her lips compressed. 'It—it was just sex for the sake of physical satisfaction, and . . .'

'And you're against physical satisfaction, are you?' Finch's regard suddenly turned sleepy, and an uncontrollable shiver that was partly attraction, partly apprehension, played up and down Blythe's spine. 'You're going to tell me you regret this too, are you?' His mouth, warm and vibrant, captured hers before she could evade it, his tongue teasing her lips apart even as she sought to deny it entrance, to probe, stroke, excite, until she moaned helplessly and knew she was kissing him back.

Half pinned beneath him, Blythe could feel his muscled body stretched the full length of hers, virile, enticing. His lips began to trace a fevered path down her throat, and she gave an anguished shiver as his fingers moved leisurely over to cup and caress her suddenly aching breasts, shaping their swelling contours to his hands, to his tormenting mouth.

'Well?' Finch demanded tautly at length as he freed her, and Blythe shook her head wildly.

Her action was not so much in rejection of his question as in denial of the grieving sense of deprivation that was concentrating in her throbbing nipples at the removal of his mouth. God, how could she have allowed him to have such an effect on her again? She didn't even have the excuse of having had too much relaxing champagne this time! she censured herself derisively. Couldn't she see that he was merely using her to slake a basic hunger? And she, God help her, was co-operatively assisting him!

What was more, the humiliating thought followed, it was entirely possible that he saw her simply as a convenient substitute for Delvene . . . exactly as she alleged she had been substituting him for Nathan the night before! However, the thought, no matter how mortifying, did at least enable her to resolutely quell her unruly feelings and accelerated pulse rate sufficiently to affect a dismissive shrug.

'I wasn't disputing your sexual prowess, Finch,' she told him in faintly mocking tones. 'I was simply regretting having been the object of it, that's all.' Moving determinedly to the side of the bed this time, she began dragging the sheet around her protectively. The fact that, when she left the bed, her use of it would leave him uncovered, she strongly doubted would cause him the slightest embarrassment.

She did have to admit to a certain surprise, though, when he made no attempt whatsoever to detain her on this occasion, but merely eased indolently on to his back, lacing his hands casually behind his head, and regarding her with

an equally unexpected hint of indulgent humour
touching his lips.

'Cat!' he chided pleasantly in a drawl. 'I might
remind you that we do happen to be married, you
know.'

'Although only for Lief's sake. No other
reason,' Blythe hastened to impress on him.

'Apart from the mention of other, future
children, of course . . . which you didn't dispute,
as I recall.'

Blythe's stomach lurched, and she scrambled
hastily from the bed. The sight of Finch's sleek
and powerful, and now totally naked body, did
nothing for her composure. He was the embodi-
ment of ultimate masculinity and, against her
will, her gaze was drawn irresistibly to the hard,
muscular lines of him, her blood immediately,
dismayingly, racing riotously through her veins.

'I—well . . .' she faltered uneasily, and ran the
tip of her tongue over her suddenly dry lips, 'I
didn't pay much attention to it. I had other things
on my mind as well at the time, and—and I doubt
I was in favour of a purely sexual relationship in
order to—produce them, anyway.'

Finch fixed her with an explicit sidelong
glance. 'Although making love is the generally
accepted method of conceiving children?' drily.

Circles of heat coloured Blythe's cheeks. 'That
wasn't what I was meaning!' she flared vexedly. 'I
just meant that—that going to bed with you is not
the type of arrangement I was envisaging . . . or
want.'

'Nevertheless, we will continue to share this bed,' Finch declared with a nonchalant arrogance that set her teeth on edge.

'And if I refuse?' She glared at him rebelliously.

The smile he sent her did little to assuage her mutinous feelings. 'Then I guess you could find it somewhat discomfiting to be carried here—kicking and screaming, as it were—every night.'

Blythe seethed, her breasts rising and falling rapidly. 'Although not if I lock myself in my own room first!'

Finch crooked an expressive brow. 'You think something as minor as a lock would deter me if I really wanted to gain access? And then only if I allow you to keep the key in the first place.' He flexed a solid shoulder, the corded sinews rippling. 'Besides, I suspect it could also prove embarrassing for you if the resulting noise happened to wake Lief and he came to investigate. I doubt he would fully grasp any explanation you might give, but more importantly . . . you know how children like to talk at school.'

From where the tale would soon be all over the valley, Blythe didn't doubt. But refusing to give ground, she eyed him half mockingly, half balefully. 'And maybe it would serve you right if everyone did know that you were forcing your poor wife—who only married you for the sake of her nephew—to submit to your unwelcome physical demands,' she purred.

'Well, forcing you into my bed, anyway,' Finch

amended meaningfully, his lips twitching, and Blythe felt her face crimson.

Damn and double damn him! she railed silently, and cursed herself too, for having generously provided the ammunition with which to defeat her. How could she dare take the chance on him not saying something similar if the subject should ever happen to arise? That would be just too embarrassing to be endured!

'I still wouldn't rely on that if I were you, Finch,' she retorted finally in her haughtiest, frostiest tone. It was the only challenge he had really left her able to issue. Then turning her back on him in dismissal, she swept from the room with as much dignity as she could manage in view of her cumbersome covering.

CHAPTER SEVEN

'YOU'LL BE all right?' Finch hazarded of Blythe before taking his departure for the high country one Friday afternoon some six weeks later, and she nodded reassuringly.

This weekend it was his and Jarred's turn to take salt up to their cattle in the mountains, and although Finch had left for the same reason before, this was the first time she had been left completely on her own. Even Lief would be absent on this occasion because he was staying with a school friend for the weekend. In such a close community, the children often stayed at one another's houses, and Blythe herself had frequently had care of an extra one or two.

'Well, you know where to go if you should need any help,' Finch continued as she accompanied him to the veranda steps. 'Nicol and Brent expect to be home most of the time, and Verna and Price said they definitely would be.'

'It's OK, I can manage . . . really,' Blythe insisted with a half-laugh. 'And even without Lief to remind me, I promise not to forget to water the vegetables, or to feed the dogs, the cats, the chooks, or the pigs, etcetera.'

Finch shook his head dismissively. 'It wasn't

them I was thinking about . . . it was you. You're from the city and you're not used to being entirely alone and so far from your nearest neighbour.'

'Then I guess it's time I did become accustomed to it,' she proposed softly, touched by his concern. Adding in a wry tone, 'It will be good practice for me for when you all muster the cattle out of the high country and you're away for a week or more. It's not long now until that happens, is it?' The preparations for the muster had already begun, she knew. Horses were being checked and new shoes fitted; saddles, halters, bridles, pack frames, scrutinised, repaired or replaced.

'Another couple of weeks . . . provided the weather holds,' Finch supplied, his eyes automatically scanning the sky over the mountains, just as she had seen him do increasingly for the last month. 'Otherwise it could be sooner. The only predictable thing about the weather up there is its unpredictability, and if the snow comes early . . .' He gave an explicit shrug.

Meaning, it would then become a race against time to muster the cattle off 'the tops', as the high plains were known locally, before they became trapped, Blythe deduced from having heard the family discussing such matters.

'So this is the last time salt will be taken up, then?'

'Uh-huh! But if we're to reach the hut and unload before dark, I guess I'd better be making tracks,' he proposed, and began descending the steps. At the bottom he turned to look up at her. 'We'll probably be back late Sunday . . . OK?'

Blythe nodded, her mouth curving in response as he gave a typical tug on the brim of his hat in salute before following after Jarred, who had taken his leave only minutes previously, to the truck that was already loaded with their horses and other necessities.

However, as her gaze remained focused on her husband's tall figure, so too did Blythe's thoughts concentrate on him. As each day passed, she came to know him a little better, and she had to admit that as a husband and father-figure, if not an actual father, he was undoubtedly better than most. Oh, he could be rock-like in his determination when he set his mind to it, and certainly he was infuriating at times—purposely so on occasion where she was concerned, at least, she suspected—but for the most part he was kind, fair, easy-going, and possessed of a dry sense of humour that she found decidedly attractive.

That she was also uncomfortably aware that she was by no means unattracted to the man himself, Blythe also had to acknowledge, as much as she disliked facing the fact. It seemed a betrayal of Nathan somehow and, as a result, she did her best to squash the feeling immediately it arose. Finch was replacing Nathan on a purely physical level, that was all, she told herself resolutely.

The sound of a vehicle horn roused her from her musings with a start, and she raised her arm instinctively in farewell on seeing the truck head for the road, then turned slowly and re-entered the house.

Inside, Blythe absently went about making preparations for dinner, her thoughts still introspective. Their marriage seemed to have settled into an easy domesticity, and she supposed she was content. After the disconcerting events of their wedding night, she had viewed the notion of their sleeping together in something akin to panic, the unfamiliar and uncontrollable responses Finch had engendered both flustering and alarming her.

But strangely, he had made no move to even touch her since, despite their sharing the same bed. Every night for the first week or so, she had huddled tensely at the very edge of the bed, her nerves stretched to breaking point, her body stiff with trepidation and feverishly aware of his nearness as she waited for the contact that never came. Instead, he had exhibited no sign of even being conscious she was there, so that while she lay awake, unbearably sensitive to every agonisingly long minute that passed, he seemed totally unaware of her agitated state, and slept calmly, his breathing maddeningly regular and undisturbed.

After a time, Blythe had begun to suspect vexedly that he was deliberately keeping her on tenterhooks, in repayment for her having said she wasn't interested in any physical relationship between them. Or could it be an even more subtle form of retaliation? she wondered. An attempt, by denying her an outlet for them, to force her to acknowledge that her body did indeed have purely sexual desires of its own, regardless of her protestations. And maybe he was right, the shaming speculation had come. For how else could she explain the growing ache that pervaded her limbs, the shocking feeling of sheer wanting, that had assailed her on those recent occasions when she had awoken during the night and, to her dismay, found herself nestling against Finch's warm and powerful length?

A sudden heat flooded Blythe's cheeks, and she thrust the memories away swiftly. To be dwelling on such matters obviously meant she didn't have enough to occupy her mind, she decided, and leaving the dinner preparations, she set off to feed the animals instead. Remembering what feed, and how much was respectively required, would surely preclude any extraneous thoughts for a time, at least.

After lunch on Sunday, Blythe decided to do some gardening—the roses needed pruning and the borders along the fence urgently required weeding—but she had only just collected the necessary implements from one of the outbuildings when she heard the phone ringing, and depositing the tools on the verandah, she hurried into the homestead to answer it. With both Finch and Lief absent, she discovered she was becoming eager for the sound of another voice.

Nevertheless, the voice she heard on picking up the receiver wasn't one she had remotely expected, and it showed in her surprised response.

'Nathan! You're the last person I expected to be calling.'

'I don't see why. We're still friends, aren't we?' he countered with soft persuasiveness.

'Yes, of course. I just wasn't anticipating . . .' She broke off, shaking her head. 'Why *are* you ringing, anyway?'

'Is it so unbelievable that, missing you as I do, I might just want to talk to you?'

Blythe caught her breath. 'But what if . . . Finch had answered?'

'And what if he had!' A challenging edge entered Nathan's voice. 'I mean, your marriage is only one of convenience, after all. It's not as if you mean anything to him, except as a mother to the boy. So why shouldn't I ring you? It's nothing to him, surely, who you speak to.'

'I—I suppose not,' she faltered, an unaccountable feeling of depression washing over her at his words. 'So what did you want to talk to me about?'

'Well, as a matter of fact, I was hoping I might be able to see you.'

'See me?' she repeated with a perplexed frown.

'Yes.' There was a slight pause. 'As it happens, I'm . . . in Omeo.' He went on quickly, a trifle sardonically. 'And understandably not wishing to conduct any meeting in the presence of that arrogant husband of yours—you know how I feel about him!—I thought you might meet me here . . . or in Yuroka, if you prefer.'

'Oh, but . . .' On the point of telling him Finch

wasn't there, Blythe suddenly decided against it, knowing how Finch felt about him in return. Although Nathan apparently attributed her hesitation to another reason entirely.

'You are allowed to make your own decisions, I presume,' he put forward caustically.

'Naturally.' Her reply was defensively stiff.

'So you'll meet me here?' His voice turned anxious. 'Or shall I . . .'

'No, I'll meet you in Omeo . . . at the hotel on the hill,' she interjected quickly, guessing what he had been about to suggest, and knowing there was less chance of her being recognised in that town.

She didn't want to be seen with Nathan in Yuroka, she realised, because she felt inexplicably guilty about planning to meet him, and yet she didn't know why she should feel that way. After all, Finch and Delvene hadn't stopped talking to one another just because he was married to someone else, so why shouldn't she meet Nathan?

Notwithstanding her rationalisation, the feeling remained with her, however. Although as she drove to Omeo a short time later, it was coupled to another reason as well. She had experienced absolutely no thrill on hearing Nathan's voice, she recognised uncomfortably; only astonishment and that niggling sense of unease.

But then, on presently going into the hotel lounge and being eagerly greeted by Nathan, nor was she conscious of any great heightening of her feelings at the sight of him either, she was forced to acknowledge disappointedly. No doubt as a result of the completely unwarranted guilt she felt at being there, and which seemed to override every other consideration, she reassured herself determinedly, testily, as she allowed Nathan to guide her to a seat near the window before ordering them something to drink.

She still couldn't help being thankful the lounge was only sparsely patronised, regardless, and by no one she immediately recognised. Although as the afternoon progressed that didn't remain the case and, to her vexation, her nervousness increased in proportion to the numbers present. She wasn't doing anything wrong, so what did she have to feel guilty about?

At the same time, she was conscious of the passing hours and, not wanting to be absent when Finch returned—not having expected to be away so long, she hadn't even left a note to say when she would be back—she began to make suggestions about leaving.

'Oh, but you can't go yet,' Nathan promptly entreated urgently, clasping her hands across the table. 'It's been great seeing you and talking over old times, but . . .' he paused and drew a deep breath, 'that wasn't the only—or even the real reason I came.'

Blythe gazed at him askance, twin creases furrowing her brow. 'Then what was?'

He shrugged deprecatorily. 'I—well, the boy must be settled in fully with his relatives now——' he hesitated briefly again before continuing in more forceful accents, 'and, in consequence, not really need you any more. You could get a divorce, and then we could marry . . . as we always planned.'

Stunned by the unexpectedness of his suggestion, Blythe hardly knew what to say. 'But—but once you've committed yourself to marriage, the law expects you to remain married for a year, at least,' she stammered.

Nathan shook his head. 'Not when the marriage hasn't been consummated,' he declared triumphantly.

Blythe swallowed and, surreptitiously extricating her hands from his, dropped her gaze self-consciously to the glasses on the table. 'Except that . . . I'm afraid that doesn't apply in this case,' she disclosed reluctantly in a throaty murmur.

Nathan's nostrils flared, his whole expression one of seething fury. 'You mean the contemptible bastard's already forced himself on you?' he grated.

Blythe squirmed discomfitedly, and rued the innate honesty that couldn't allow her to let his supposition stand. 'Well . . . not exactly,' she said faintly. 'It was the night of our wedding, and—and it just sort of . . . happened.'

'In other words, you accommodated him willingly, is that what you're saying?'

Both wincing at, and objecting to, his choice of words, Blythe angled her head higher, her eyes holding his irately censuring gaze challengingly. 'If that's how you care to put it,' she allowed on a cool note, and Nathan's expression changed immediately.

'Oh, hell, I'm sorry, love. I didn't really mean it,

he apologised, seeking to make amends. He moved his chair closer and took hold of one of her hands again. 'I was just out of my mind at the thought of him touching you, of the two of you . . .' He shook his head as if to rid himself of the painful images, and when next he spoke his voice was threaded with urgent enthusiasm. 'Anyhow, in spite of all that, you can still separate from him and wait the year out.' Placing an arm about her shoulders to draw her even nearer, he coaxed close to her ear, 'You'll do that—for me—won't you?'

Aware that they were already engendering some curious glances from the hotel's other patrons—*had* she met a couple of those men at the bar before; did *they* know just whose wife she was?—Blythe tried embarrassedly to ease from beneath his arm, but to no avail. It seemed that, once having become so uncharacteristically demonstrative in public, he had no intention of releasing her.

'I—I'm sorry, but I can't,' she refused at length, and was stunned by the sudden discovery that she simply wasn't interested in resuming their relationship. 'Lief does still . . .'

'Need you?' Nathan cut in to deduce. Cupping her face with his hands, he went on hoarsely, 'He couldn't possibly, as much as I do! God, have you any idea how much I've missed you, how much I've wanted you back?' With a totally uncharacteristic lack of control, he set his mouth ardently to hers before she could even guess his intentions, let alone circumvent them.

Unable to move her head away, Blythe tried to

push him away instead, but when that was unsuccessful she had no option but to wait for his spurt of passion to expend itself, if she wasn't to make them the cynosure of all eyes by really putting up a fight. As it was, she already suspected from the sudden drop in the level of conversation around them that they weren't altogether unobserved, and she burnt with humiliation at the knowledge.

Then at last Nathan was relinquishing possession of her lips, and she immediately turned her head away to ensure he couldn't capture them again . . . and stared straight into the rigidly set and uncompromising features of her husband.

He stood no more than ten or twelve feet away, his face as hard and cold as an icefloe. But his eyes! They were a glittering, blazing emerald that scorched her from head to toe! Oh, dear God, I think he's going to strangle me! gulped Blythe in a panic, the colour that had been suffusing her face now draining away to leave it ashen.

He looked as if he were some dangerously constrained force about to explode, and only just realising her hands were still resting against Nathan's shoulders, she removed them with frantic haste and started to her feet as her husband began advancing towards them with determined strides.

'Finch . . . !' She held out a tentative hand that could have been in placation or for self-protection. 'It's not what . . .'

'You deceitful little bitch!' he broke in on her to denounce in a grating undertone. Fastening his fingers about her wrist in a bone-crushing grip, he propelled her past him, in the direction of the door. 'I'll see to *you* at home!'

Valiantly doing her best to overcome the shiver of apprehension that rippled along her spine, Blythe still turned back to him urgently. 'But if you would just . . .'

'Go home, Blythe! *Now!*' Finch interrupted once more to order furiously between clenched teeth.

Wary of provoking him even further, and already feeling unbearably embarrassed by the whole eipsode—if those present hadn't known who she was before, she was positive they did now!—Blythe acquiesced defeatedly and started for the door, although it took every ounce of willpower she possessed to keep her head high as she did so. Behind her, Finch's voice rasped on her nerves as he promptly turned his attention to Nathan.

'While as for you, you sneaking, obnoxious mongrel . . . ! I suggest you get the hell out of here . . . while you're still in one piece!'

Unable to refrain from at least glancing over her shoulder, Blythe saw Nathan flush and push to his own feet. 'You can't tell me what to do, Carmody!' he disputed, albeit in somewhat blustering tones, as he eyed the taut lines of the other man's menacing form. 'If I want to see Blythe, and she wants to see me, why we shouldn't meet? She is my ex-fiancée, after all!'

'She was never your fiancée!' Finch all but snarled at him. 'But she is *my wife*! So if you know what's good for you . . . !'

Blythe hurried on, out of earshot, knowing that Nathan had a healthy regard for his own safety and, consequently, was unlikely to chance ignoring Finch's second warning. But it was only as she made her way past the bar that she realised that Jarred had accompanied Finch—and that, to her despair, his expression was censuring as well.

'Jarred, it wasn't how it looked,' she tried to impress on him in a whisper, pausing beside him. She couldn't have passed without at least attempting to explain.

In response, he gave an impassive shrug. 'It's none of my business what you do.'

'Although that still doesn't prevent you from disapproving,' she stated the obvious with a sigh.

Jarred's mouth shaped sardonically. 'Finch isn't exactly unknown in these parts—as you're damned well aware—and you sure didn't exactly do much for his reputation, or his pride, by letting yourself be seen kissing another man so—enthusiastically, in public, did you?'

Blythe bit her lip. 'Except that I wasn't kissing him . . . enthusiastically or otherwise! He was kissing me!'

His green eyes, so like her husband's, gazed at her askance. 'Somehow I doubt if Finch was in any frame of mind to recognise such a fine distinction,' he declared drily. There was brief pause. 'The same as I suspect you wouldn't either if the circumstances were reversed.'

No, she supposed she wouldn't, Blythe was compelled to concede as all her earlier feelings of guilt returned in full force. 'I knew I should never have agreed to meet him,' she mused with a dismal shake of her head.

'But you did.'

'Yes, foolishly I did. And now . . .' Some sixth sense had her halting and spinning around, to find Finch's commanding figure approaching rapidly.

'Now comes the reckoning, I'm afraid,' put in Jarred heavily before his cousin reached them.

Blythe nodded, swallowing apprehensively, and then Finch was gripping her arm again as if he would like to break it, indicating that his fury hadn't abated one iota. Of Nathan there was no sign, she noted involuntarily, and deduced he must have prudently taken his leave already by a different exit.

'I thought I told you to go home!' Finch bit out direfully, his fingers digging deeper into her arm.

Blythe shook her head. 'I only stopped to try and—explain to Jarred,' she pushed out unsteadily.

Finch uttered a harhly derisive sound. 'You think he needed an explanation for what we saw? You made it all too damned obvious to every person here, you conniving, double-dealing bitch!'

Blythe shrank from his words, and it was left to his cousin to exhort with a doubtful frown, 'Finch . . . go easy!'

'Keep out of it, Jarred!' the warning retort came immediately as a muscle stirred dangerously beside Finch's grim jaw. 'This is between my dear treacherous wife and myself!'

Although appreciative of the younger man's

intervention, Blythe also felt obliged to veto any further efforts on her behalf with a demurring shake of her head. She didn't want to perhaps be the cause of any trouble within the family, and no matter how irate Finch was, she very much doubted she was in danger of suffering any actual harm. She had come to know her husband that well, at least.

Or she hoped she had! Blythe was forced to amend with a compulsive shiver a while later as Finch drove them home. Certainly she had never seen him this livid before, or known his anger continue undiminished for so long! He was still as taut as a newly-strung fence, his face bleak, his eyes smouldering with a hot and savage emerald fire that increased her nervousness every mile they covered. So when it became apparent that he—temporarily, at least—had no intention of breaking the tension-crackling atmosphere that sparked between them, she finally took it upon herself to venture into conciliatory speech.

'Look—I really am sorry, but . . .'

'Sorry I found out about your amorous little interlude, or sorry that I brought it to a disappointingly early finish?' Finch cut in acidly, the accompanying look he bestowed on her scathing in its contempt. 'Or maybe I didn't, at that. Maybe you'd been with him all weekend, and were just bidding your fond farewell . . . in time for you to rush home to play the part of the patiently waiting wife! Is that how it really was, Blythe? *It it?*' It was almost possible to hear his teeth grind together in his fury.

'*No!*' she denied on a strangled note, aghast. 'I didn't even speak to him until after lunch today. He telephoned . . .'

'And you couldn't wait to rush to his side!' he charged in jeering tones. 'I'm surprised you didn't invite him to the house. That would have made an even more cosy love-nest for the two of you, wouldn't it?' He paused, his strong mouth assuming a derogatory curve. 'Or didn't you want the illusory picture you've created of your so precious Nathan to be tainted by recollections of me?'

Blythe shook her head in negation. 'Since I don't have any illusory pictures of Nathan, that wouldn't have been possible, in any case,' she replied with studied control. 'The reason I didn't invite him to the house was that I didn't think *you* would like the idea of him being there.'

'But you thought I *would* like the idea of you sneaking off to make love to him in public instead!'

'We weren't making love!' she flared.

'I arrived too soon for it to actually progress that far, did I?' Finch now switched his attack, sarcastically. 'How very frustrating for him!'

'In view of the face that making love to him was never my intention, not at all!' And with a sigh, 'Besides, I've already told you how Nathan regards such—such behaviour without the benefit of marriage.'

Finch pressed his lips tight. 'I also know what my own eyes tell me!' he ground out corrosively. 'That now you're someone else's wife, he suddenly wants what he ignored before!' He inhaled deeply, his emerald eyes ranging over her with insolent disparagement. 'And you were only too willingly offering him encouragement, weren't you, my sweet?'

Colour poured into Blythe's cheeks. 'That's not true!' she disclaimed with hoarse urgency. 'I wasn't encouraging him! I wasn't even kissing him, in fact. *He* was kissing me! And then only because I didn't realise he meant to.' Her wide grey eyes clung beseechingly to his hard, set profile. 'Finch . . . please! You have to believe that!'

'Do I?' The glance he spared her was derisively disdainful. 'Then why meet him at all? Supposedly, just so you could hold hands and commiserate with each other?' He gave a short, scoffing laugh that jarred her nerves as he brought the car to a halt, and Blythe was surprised to discover they had reached the homestead. Now Finch turned in his seat to face her directly, and her eyes dilated apprehensively as she instinctively shrank from the roiling emotions still reflected in his tight-lipped expression. 'Don't play me for a fool, Blythe!' he rasped rawly. 'Do you think I don't know you met him in Omeo because you thought there was less chance of anyone recognising you there . . . less chance of *me* finding out!' The knuckles of the hand still gripping the steering wheel whitened. 'So tell me . . . just how many other times have you gone behind my back to meet him there?'

Blythe's lips parted. Was that what he thought? *'None!'* Her answer was voiced on a gasped note. 'Today was the first time I've seen him since I was last in Geelong! Besides, how could there have been other times? Lief's always been here with me before, even if you weren't.'

'Except when he was at school, of course!' with trenchant pungency.

Blythe's jaw lifted, her own temper beginning to rise now. She might have been willing to concede that he had some cause for displeasure regarding the afternoon's happenings, but that didn't mean she was also about to meekly accept any other accusations he cared to make.

'Then why don't you ask around, if that's what you believe? Someone would surely have seen me, wouldn't they?' she returned with some asperity. 'Moreover, and no matter what you think, I did only meet Nathan in order to talk. Nothing else!' Thrusting open the car door, she alighted in a resentful movement.

A fraction of a second later Finch had followed suit. 'You expect me to believe that?' he demanded scornfully, moving around the vehicle with a forceful stride. 'After the scene that met my eyes when I walked into that damned hotel?'

'I've already told you that wasn't supposed to happen!'

'Well, doubtless not with your husband watching, at least! And despite your protestations, I noticed you weren't exactly fighting him off!' His lips curled. 'How could you, while your hands were clinging to him so lovingly?'

'They weren't clinging to him!' Blythe repudiated fiercely. 'If you'd bothered to look a little closer before jumping to conclusions . . .'

'*Jumping* to conclusions!' Finch interposed incredulously, harshly. 'You seem to have forgotten that you happen to be *my* wife, and as such, you shouldn't have been in that sly bastard's arms in the first place! Either in or out of public!'

Blythe shifted from one foot to the other discomfitedly and, in defence, recklessly hurried into gibing speech. 'And that's what this is really all about, isn't it? Just because I dared to meet Nathan, all your possessive male instincts are on the rampage, even though our marriage isn't a normal one!' She about-turned angrily and started for the homestead.

'Then perhaps it would have been advisable if you'd considered that before sneaking off to see him!' Finch ground out behind her.

'I didn't sneak . . .' She broke off with a startled exclamation on abruptly finding herself being snatched off her feet by inflexible arms that kept her bound to a hard chest as Finch continued on towards the house at a determined pace, notwithstanding her immediate squirming efforts to escape. 'Put me down!' she half demanded, half panted. 'What do you think you're doing?'

'I'm about to correct the mistake you appear to be labouring under, as to just where your loyalties are supposed to lie!' Suddenly there was a sensuous cast to his mouth, a certain intensity in his green eyes, that stole her breath and had her heart thudding against her ribs in alarm as he strode purposefully across the veranda and into the homestead. 'From now on there'll be no more pretensions in either our marriage . . . or our bed, my sweet! Nor do I intend there to be room in your mind for any more thoughts of your damn Nathan, because I mean to obliterate them, once and for all . . . starting right now!' he vowed roughly, shouldering open the door to their bedroom and making for the bed.

There was no mistaking his intention, and Blythe's eyes widened in indignation and panic, her struggles becoming more furious. Then before she knew it, she was lying on the bed, pinned beneath him, his muscular length crushing her against the yielding softness of the mattress. She tried to push him away, but he trapped her hands between them, his mouth coming down on hers, hard and demanding, to silence her half-uttered frantic protests.

Finch held her tightly, his tongue stabbing, probing, deeper and deeper within her soft mouth, his hands tracing every curving inch of her with an insolently knowing touch that ignited a smouldering flame of traitorous desire even as she tried desperately to deny it. The humiliating knowledge had Blythe moving frenziedly, doubling her efforts to be free, and at last succeeding in dragging her lips from the devastating contact of his.

'Finch . . . please!' she entreated throatily. 'Don't

do this to us!'

Above his sable-framed eyes, a dark brow arched ironically. 'I wasn't aware we were an "us",' he growled. And on a deepening note, 'But we're going to be from now on, believe me!' His lips claimed hers again, taking her mouth by storm, but this time with a slow, persuasive hunger that was like nothing she had ever experienced before as it aroused responsive, consuming emotions that she fought against desperately.

Not that it seemed to make any difference how much she fought, for her senses appeared to have a will of their own, so that eventually she was forced to acknowledge that it wasn't Finch she was fighting, but her own desires.

She tried to tell herself that her husband was merely unleashing the feelings that had been stimulated by her meeting with Nathan; that she was simply transferring them to Finch, that was all; but as a warm ache started to fan out from her stomach to course to her very extremities and she arched instinctively to meet his stirring caresses, she knew she couldn't continue deceiving herself any longer.

It wasn't Nathan she was in love with, but her husband. It was as simple as that, and at last she could admit the reason for those moments of awareness that had so disturbed her. She had been attracted to Finch from the first day they met. Now she also knew why there had been no heightening of her feelings when Nathan rang her, when she saw him . . . and why his impassioned kiss had engendered no other emotion but embarrassment for his choice of venue. No, Nathan had never managed to strike that vital chord within her as Finch had, to bring to life such deep and fervent emotions.

And now she had conceded as much, it was as if a dam had burst within Blythe, and she gave herself up fully and freely to the exciting sensations her husband was arousing, her arms closing around his broad shoulders, her body moving beneath his in open invitation as she returned his kisses uninhibitedly.

She wanted to feel her skin pressed against the naked hardness of his instead of the clothes that kept her at a distance from the provocative touch of his muscular body, wanted to feel again the warmth of him surging deep inside her, to please him as he was pleasing her, and to hell with the reason that had finally brought her back into his arms once more!

Mercifully, Finch seemed to divine her wishes, for his hands moved to the buttons of her blouse, swiftly relieving her of it along with the rest of her garments until she lay bare to his heated gaze. But when his hands quickly went to his own clothes, she impetuously caught at his arm to stop him.

'No . . . let me,' she whispered huskily, a trifly shyly, but swivelling on to her knees beside him, her fingers reaching for the front of his shirt.

Finch drew an audible breath, his gaze, dark and smoky with desire, slamming into hers as her fingers began their task. At least his earlier anger had disappeared, Blythe was able to note gratefully, although momentarily she still thought he might prevent her continuing when his eyes narrowed slightly in suspicion. He didn't, however, but sat tautly, if watchfully, and as still as a statue apart from the sharp rise and fall of his chest that denoted the force of his feelings.

With his shirt unfastened, Blythe eased it from his shoulders with infinite slowness, her hands following its downward slide savouringly as they glided over smoothly ridged upper muscles to the hair-roughened, sinewed forearms below. When the material dropped from him altogether, she discarded it carelessly, her fingers then retracing their path back to his shoulders to explore the width of them evocatively, before gradually edging lower where they lingered leisurely over his powerful chest, and then took their time descending to the hard flatness of his stomach.

He had an impressive body, strong, vigorously male and very fit, and she loved being able to caress the tanned skin, to inflame his senses with her touch as much as it did hers. And her touch did arouse him, Blythe knew. She could hear his breathing becoming harsher, more unsteady, the tension emanating from him almost tangibly as she pleasurably prolonged the experience.

Catching her head between his hands, Finch set her away from him with a tortured groan.

'What are you trying to do to me, you little witch?' he muttered thickly. Then, with his flaring eyes delving intently into hers, 'Who the hell taught you to do that?'

Blythe flushed at the distrust in his voice, her glossy lashes dropping swiftly to hide the thorn of pain it caused. Did he really believe she had responded quite so boldly to any man before? Surely he realised that since most of her adult life had revolved around Lief, there had been little time for any men, apart from Nathan.

'You did,' she replied softly at length with feigned calm. She caught at her lip with even white teeth, continuing to avoid his gaze self-consciously. 'Didn't you like it?'

Finch's fingers sank deeper into her hair. 'You know damn well I did!' he growled on a raw note. 'How could I not?' As if he was unable to help himself, his mouth found hers in a fiery, crushing demand that erased every extraneous thought from her mind except her mounting need of him. 'But now I think it's time I repaid the compliment . . .' he continued in a horse murmur against the parted softness of her clinging lips and, within seconds, had divested himself of the remainder of his clothing with considerably less languor than Blythe had his shirt.

Gathering her back into his arms, he lowered them both to the pillows again, his muscular legs entwining sensuously with hers, his hands and lips rousing, intoxicating, as they moved over her, searing her from her throat to her thighs, and making her tremble from the unbridled feelings he was stirring within her and the feverish desire to once again know his possession . . .

Afterwards too limp and spent to move, Blythe remained collapsed against the pillows when Finch eased away from her, and for a time the only sound heard in the room was that of their gradually decelerating breathing. Then Finch propped himself up on an elbow, and when she turned her head languidly to look at him, Blythe was surprised, and dismayed, to see that a vestige of his prior tension had returned to his face.

'And don't bother telling me you regretted that too,' he drawled in a somewhat sardonic vein, reminding her of her comments after their wedding night. 'Because we both know differently, don't we, my sweet?' He quirked a meaningful brow.

Blythe reddened and averted her gaze. No, she couldn't claim to have regretted it, her own spontaneous action in undressing him had certainly given the lie to that. Conversely, though, she found she couldn't bring herself to divulge either that her responses had been born of love. In view of the events of the afternoon, she strongly doubted he would believe her—indeed it had come as a unexpected and mind-shattering revelation to herself—but worse, he might reject her love as unwanted, or even find it amusing considering how persistently she had professed her feelings for Nathan, not to mention providing him with a hold over her that could prove devastating. After all, his reversal of demeanour now surely demonstrated just how untouched his emotions really were, precisely as Nathan had declared, she recalled, when he had claimed that she meant nothing to Finch except as a mother to Lief. No, notwithstanding being his wife, she was still just a woman, whom he merely wanted as such, and she would do well to remember that, she decided.

Steeling herself to return his gaze calmly, Blythe now forced an indifferent shrug. 'And as I've said before, I don't dispute your sexual prowess, Finch,' she said finally, tightly. 'Just your wish, or imagined right, to keep demonstrating it.'

'Although it's acceptable for you to practise your seductive arts when the mood takes you, I gather,' he promptly retorted with a mocking edge.

Knowing exactly what he was referring to, Blythe reddened anew. 'I—I was simply attempting to—to thwart your efforts to exert total male dominance,' she blustered.

'How interesting!' Finch's tone turned silky, and immediately had an apprehensive tremor chasing up her spine as a result. 'That should add some spice to our nights, at least.'

Blythe sat up swiftly. 'Except there aren't going to be any such nights!' she tried to impress on him in a panic. How could she stand it, knowing his actions were governed by nothing but a fundamental physical need?

'The hell there aren't!' Finch clipped out on a roughening note. 'For six weeks now I've tried taking my time with you, not rushing you, and all the while you've been playing me for a pigeon behind my back!'

'No, I . . .'

'Well, not any more!' he went on as if she hadn't tried to speak. 'In future we'll be making love whenever I decide!'

Blythe's eyes flashed as anger flared. 'That's not making love! That's just having sex!' she slated.

'Call it what you like,' Finch returned, flexing an unperturbed shoulder. 'You started the play . . . now it's time for you to pay.'

But just what would the final cost be? Blythe speculated despairingly. Somehow she suspected this could be one of those times when ignorance *was* bliss.

CHAPTER EIGHT

'Oh, I wish I could go with them too, Blythe, don't you?' Lief exclaimed on a wistful note as he brought Star competently to a halt beside her and Nerida.

The girls were sitting on a hay bale in the late afternoon autumn sunshine, watching as Nerida's brothers loaded the truck with an assortment of gear—horse feed, swags, camp ovens and billies, spare stirrups and leather, axes, saddles, provisions for themselves, among them—ready for the muster that would see them departing the following morning, along with every other cattleman in the valley who also grazed stock in the mountains.

The horses, together with the food Blythe had already cooked in preparation, would be loaded shortly before they left, and then it would all be driven via logging and fire trails until they were high in the ranges. To reach the high plains on the very top of the divide, though, everything would then have to be transferred to packhorses for the climb to the Carmodys' hut.

There were a number of such huts scattered throughout the mountains—for the most part erected some decades previously—and through the years they had become an institution. Originally built by the cattlemen to provide not only shelter while mustering stock but also a store for their equipment, despite being of only basic construction—roughly hewn timber or corrugated iron, with stone fireplaces—because the cattlemen were willing to share them with all, they were never locked, or without a supply of fundamental food and dry matches, and therefore provided an often life-saving haven for bushwalkers caught in summer storms, and skiers during winter blizzards.

Now, as Blythe's gaze lifted to her nephew's, she smiled to see the obvious yearning on his face, and was amazed once again at the change that had been wrought in him in such a short time. Sitting bareback on his mount—the general consensus being that it was the best way to learn to ride because one attained greater balance—he seemed so much a part of his surroundings that it would have been possible to assume he had never lived anywhere else.

Her early fears that he might not have taken to the outdoor life had certainly been made a mockery of, she mused wryly, while, partly through his nights away from home, he was beginning to display a confidence, an independence, she sometimes found difficult to credit.

'Mmm, I suppose it could be quite interesting to see,' she allowed finally, but in protectively dispassionate accents. When all was said and done, Finch hadn't even so much as asked if she might also care to learn to ride—a necessary accomplishment for attending the muster—she reflected moodily. No doubt he would be happier with Delvene's company! the waspish conclusion immediately ensued, for she knew that the girl, along with Nerida and some others from the valley, would be taking part. However, to Lief she merely consoled, 'Never mind, at least Finch said you'll get your chance in a year or two, when you're a good enough rider, to accompany them when they take the cattle into the mountains at the start of summer.'

'By which time Pixie will be able to go with you as well,' put in Nerida, eyeing the pup that lay nearby and which followed Lief just about everywhere these days. 'Finch told me she's coming along really well.'

Lief nodded, smiling happily, his attention temporarily diverted from muster. 'Yes, she already knows "sit", "stay", and "come behind",' he relayed proudly. 'And when we took her into the paddock with a couple of the older dogs the other day so she could watch them working the other cattle, you could see she was really keen to work with them.'

'That's very good,' praised Nerida sincerely. 'She sounds as if she'll be a great help in the years to come. Good dogs, especially "find" dogs, are a vital part of any mustering team, and will save you hours of hard work in the moutains.'

' "Find" dogs?' Blythe queried, unfamiliar

with the term. Since coming to the valley she had learnt of leaders and heelers: the former those dogs that instinctively went to the head of the moving cattle to not only lead them in the right direction down from the mountains, but also to slow them if they showed a tendency to move too fast; the latter ensuring that the cattle kept moving in a closely controlled bunch—with the added persuasion of a sharp nip on the heel for those that showed signs of lagging.

'They're the ones that will find the cattle for you,' supplied Lief knowledgeably.

While Nerida detailed, 'Mmm, when you're in thick scrub, or rough and heavily timbered country, they pick up the stock's scent, dash off to find them and bail them up, barking like mad, until you come to relieve them of their find. You can hear them from miles away.' The last was added with a laugh.

Blythe nodded. 'I see,' she acknowledged, albeit somewhat flatly, doubting she would ever get to see any of them in action.

Evidently believing her tone to have been caused by something else, Nerida looked at her sidelong, questioning as Lief departed in order to join the men now, 'Doesn't the thought of the high plains and the muster do anything for you, like it does for the rest of us?'

Blythe averted her gaze slightly, her eyes coming to rest on the tree-covered mountains in the distance. The same mountains Finch scanned watchfully every day now, looking for that tint of brown in the clouds that could presage snow. The weather was much cooler of late, even though the days were still sunny and filled with the warm fragrance of gum trees, grass, and earth. The nights were cold, though, and the valley shrouded in mist in the early mornings, the poplars and oaks that lined the road turning gold and red, their leaves beginning to fall.

'Since I've never seen either, I couldn't really say,' she answered carefully at last.

Nerida's brows lifted. 'But you would *like* to see them?'

'Oh, yes! Very much, as a matter of fact.' Blythe was surprised, and a little disconcerted, by the vehemence of her impulsive reply, and immediately set about tempering it. She didn't want everyone to know Finch hadn't even cared to make the possibility a likelihood for her. 'But of course, I don't ride,' she excused herself with what she hoped was a sufficient note of finality, as if that settled the matter.

Luckily, Nerida seemed to view it that way too, for she simply nodded ruefully in understanding and commented, 'Well, maybe you'll be able to see them some other time, then, when you've learnt to ride.' She went on enthusiastically, 'Delvene and I love the musters, and we've never missed a year since we were first allowed to go. Of course, none of the men have either,' she added with a laugh, 'and for Dad, that's more than forty years. Mum used to go as well, but she doesn't do much riding these days, so she stays home now.' Halting, she eyed Blythe quizzically. 'Talking of Delvene, though, you didn't mind me bringing her here so Finch could shoe her horse for her, I hope?' She lifted a shoulder uneasily. 'I mean, in view of their—er—previous relationship. But when her mount suddenly threw a show this morning, I naturally thought of the forge here as being the closest, because hand-made shoes do fit so much better than ready-made ones.'

Blythe's nails dug into the palms of her hands. 'No, of course I didn't mind,' she dissembled with pseudo-indifference, her features studiously schooled.

In fact, the old forge in one of the outbuildings was where Finch and Delvene were now, and doubtless deep in conversation, she supposed. Probably about their times together, before she and Lief had come along to throw a spanner in the works, she surmised with an inner grimace. But as much as it cost her to remain where she was, her pride wouldn't allow her to interrupt them, despite the almost painful desire to do just that. That it was plain old-fashioned jealousy gnawing at her, Blythe knew, but unfortunately that still didn't make it any easier to bear.

Instead, she made herself continued with her charade by shrugging and countering as offhandedly as possible, 'Why *should* I mind? After all, surely everyone realises that Finch and I only married for Lief's sake? Not—not for any of the normally accepted reasons.'

Unexpectedly, Nerida eyed her somewhat strangely at that. 'Meaning, you wouldn't care if they continued their—association?'

Blythe's heart contracted at the thought. 'I—well—I don't know I would go so far as to say that,' she stammered jerkily. 'There are appearances to be considered. If—if only for Lief's sake,' came the camouflaging afterthought.

'Well, I can't see you having any worries on that score where Finch is concerned, in any event,' Nerida proposed in a lighter tone. 'He's nothing if not loyal, and he certainly wouldn't have entered into the convention of marriage lightly, I know.'

Blythe allowed the remark to pass without comment. In lieu, hoping to divert the conversation by declaring with simulated brightness, she said, 'And marriages in the valley seem to be coming thick and fast at the moment. It's not long now until both you and Jarred marry, is it?' The latter had been engaged to a girl from Omeo for some time now.

'No, only a matter of weeks, in fact,' confirmed Nerida, her happiness evident, and easily distracted by such a subject.

And why wouldn't she be happy? mused Blythe, when Russ made it obvious he was very much in love with her—sometimes to the stage where Blythe felt undeniable twinges of envy at the other girl's good fortune. She only wished Finch, just once, would look at her in the same manner Russ did Nerida.

'After the cattle sales that take place once the muster's over,' the other girl continued. 'Mine, only just over a week later, and Jarred's six weeks after that. To give Russ and me time to return from our honeymoon to attend it.' She laughed. 'We wouldn't want to miss his wedding now that he's finally decided to take the plunge. All the same, though . . .' her face sobered again and she grimaced, 'I wish I didn't have to miss the first couple of days of the muster in order to have a fitting for my dress. But Aunt Claire says it's imperative, and since she's giving up her time to make it for me, I suppose I shall just have to grin and bear it.' She sighed resignedly.

'You won't be leaving with the others in the morning, then?' Blythe's brows arched in surprise.

'No, I'll be going later. Dad will take my gear up . . . all except Gem, of course.' Gem being her horse, Blythe presumed. 'I'll take her in our smaller truck.' Nerida's lips shaped ruefully. 'Delvene's been teasing me something awful about missing . . . oh, there she is now!' she broke off to exclaim on seeing her friend and Finch emerge from the shed and move to the horse tethered outside. 'Finch must be ready to fit the shoe.' Then, with a grin at Blythe, 'I bet you were surprised to find you were marrying a blacksmith as well as a cattleman.'

'A little,' Blythe conceded absently, her gaze focused on the two by the shed, and all her senses rebelling against their smiling familiarity.

'It's odd, but I never pictured Finch married to anyone else but Delvene,' Nerida put forward in a thoughtful tone, causing her companion to glance at her sharply, suspecting a malicious intent in the remark.

'Yes, well, circumstances change,' Blythe just managed to get out tautly.

Now it was Nerida who looked at her quickly, intently. However, it appeared there had been no ill-will in her comment, after all, when with a slight shake of her head, she apologised, 'I'm sorry. I wasn't meaning anything by that, you know. I guess I was just speaking my thoughts aloud.' She paused, her expression assumed a diffidence Blythe had never seen encompass her before. 'Look, I admit I wasn't in favour of your marriage to Finch at the start, but . . . well, we've always been a close family, and I really would like the two of us to be friends if it's possible.' She tilted her head to one side, half-smiling tentatively. 'Do you think it might be?'

'I'm sure it is,' Blythe had no hesitation in assuring her, relieved that the other girl's previous opposition had evidently been laid to rest. 'I'd be glad to have you as a friend.'

Nerida's smile widened immediately. 'Thank you. That makes me very pleased.' She paused, a certain self-consciousness coming back into her manner once more. 'And especially when, to tell the truth, I think you've been good for Finch. In fact, that's what really prompted my remark about Delvene,' she hurried on to explain before

Blythe could recover from the surprise of her first unexpected disclosure. 'I *did* used to think she and Finch were perfect for one another, that she would be the best wife for him, but then . . . along came you and Lief and—well, of late I've begun to have a change of heart, you might say.'

Blythe smiled gratefully. She only wished Finch could have had a change of heart too. But no, he was still as content as ever to remain conversing amiably with Delvene, even though he had now finished shoeing her horse! she noted with some acrimony.

That the feeling remained with her, despite all her attempts to subdue it, if only for the sake of her pride, was more than apparent, nevertheless, as Blythe went about her normal tasks that evening with a simmering aggression.

Not that Finch said so much as a word. He merely contemplated her idly, the suspicion of amusement she detected in his expression only rankling further, so that when it came time to prepare for bed she was as close to boiling point as she had ever been in her life.

'OK, are you going to tell me . . . or am I just supposed to guess?' Finch drawled indolently at last as he sat on the bed removing his shirt while she stormed about the room gathering up her nightwear before heading for the shower.

'Tell you what?' Blythe gritted perversely. He hadn't deigned to enquire before, so why should she rush to tell him now?

'Why you're resembling a volcano looking for somewhere to erupt,' drily.

Oh, yes, he could find it amusing! she railed inwardly. 'You can guess whatever reason you like!' she threw at him disdainfully and, whirling into the adjoining bathroom, she swung the door closed between them with a satisfyingly resounding slam. At least that provided some outlet for her pent-up feelings!

Stripping quickly, Blythe turned on the shower full force, the hot needles of spray that stung her skin when she stepped into the tiled cubicle matching the barbs of resentment that pricked at her insides. However, on reaching for the soap, she felt a draught of cool air touch her and, spinning around, gasped to find Finch shutting the glass door behind him, entrapping them in the confined space.

'Get out!' she blazed infuriatedly. 'Get out of here, Finch!' Her voice rose as all her anger and despair suddenly overflowed and she began pummelling wildly at his broad chest. 'You were happy enough with just Delvene's company this afternoon, so why don't you go and join her in her shower now, too! It's all right for you to talk and laugh with her, but I'm not allowed to even speak to Nathan!' Unbidden tears filled her eyes and mingled with the water splashing over her face. 'Well, you needn't think I'm about to be a convenient substitute for her again! If you find her so congenial, you should have married *her* ... n-not me!' A sob rose in her throat.

With humiliating ease Finch captured her beating fists, pinning them behind her with an inescapable hand as he pulled her close against his long, hard, and sensuously wet length.

'And if I'd wanted to marry her, I would have done so years ago,' he advised on a thick note, tilting her rebellious face up to his, and set his mouth to hers with a languorous, provoking expertise that had Blythe uttering an inarticulate sound in her throat and struggling against him in a desperate attempt to negate the wayward yearning that immediately beset her.

But her frantic movements only succeeded in making her more aware of him; of the stimulating feel of his powerful form; of the obvious arousal she was engendering in him; and of the mortifying rush of heat that was beginning to envelop her own body in response.

Lifting his head slightly, Finch gazed down at her with a wryly teasing smile catching at the corners of his firmly-moulded lips. 'Moreover, if that's the cause of your little flare-up, it would appear you also possess a few territorial instincts yourself, my sweet,' he murmured, stroking his fingers disturbingly against her jaw and down her throat.

Blythe trembled uncontrollably, flushing. Oh, God, he hadn't guessed why his association with Delvene had affected her so strongly, had he? Why, even now, as the water continued to cascade over them, she was unable to think clearly while pressed so close to the slippery hardness of him.

'I—well, at least I didn't flaunt Nathan under your nose!' she managed to charge at length in flustered defence.

Finch favoured her with a drily expressive glance. 'No, you went behind my back instead,' he conceded. Bending his head, he brushed his lips across hers lingeringly. 'And I, at least, didn't subject you to the display of kissing her either.'

'N-nor was I kissing Nathan!' Blythe denied, straining away from him. 'As—as I've told you before. You just refuse to believe me because it suits you to—to be able to throw it up at me whenever it's convenient.'

'Except that I've never found anything connected with Nathan even remotely convenient,' sardonically. 'Nor for that matter, Delvene either. She happens to be an acquaintance of long standing, that's all. Nothing more, nothing less.'

Blythe found it hard to believe, but more importantly, she was anxious to have him leave, and she judiciously concentrated her attention on achieving that end. 'Yes—well, if that's what you came to say, I should be pleased if you now just let me get on with my shower . . .' She eyed the door pointedly.

Ignoring the hint, he surveyed her lazily with his emerald eyes from between long, wet and spiky lashes. 'And if it wasn't all I came for?'

Blythe's heart skipped a beat and then pounded

raggedly. 'Finch, I'm getting cold . . .' she prevaricated, and then immediately regretted it when he reached for the soap and proceeded to start washing her with his free hand in slow, provocative movements.

'Then it will be my pleasure to warm you.'

Warm her? Her skin already felt as if it was burning! His hand, silky with lather, caressed her shoulder, slid lower to soap her breasts, lingering over her nipples, his fingers circling them tormentingly, rubbing over them, gently pulling on them until they ached with the desire to have his mouth take the place of his hand.

'Finch!' Her protesting voice had a strangled, hoarse sound to it. She couldn't—wouldn't—give in to his, or her own, sensuality again! 'I'm in no mood for any more games!' she choked, trying frantically once more to squirm free of the grip he still had on her wrists.

'And I'm not playing any game, my sweet,' he murmured huskily, releasing his hold on her at last, but only in order to crush her to him tightly with both arms as his head lowered to hers again.

Demandingly, his lips covered her own, and Blythe willed herself to remain unresponsive. But the natural urge of her body wouldn't heed the direction given by her brain, betraying her as her mouth parted to admit his seeking tongue, and her arms clasped involuntarily about his muscled shoulders.

Finch's hands moved to caress her wet back, playing up and down her spine, urging her hips closer to him. She could feel the tautly male outline of him impressed on her from shoulder to knee, and her body quivered from the searing sensations he was creating within her.

For a large man he was irresistibly gentle. And that was half the trouble, Blythe thought ruefully. If he had been rougher, less caring whether his lovemaking gave her pleasure or not, it would have been easier to fight him, to perhaps push him into taking her by force and thereby provide her with a reason to dislike him. But he didn't force her, he . . . he *seduced* her every time, damn him, and as a result it seemed that when she was in his arms nothing else in the world mattered!

Now, as the water continued to cascade over them, there was an unquestioning excitement in feeling his hands slide over her, a sensuousness never experienced before in the enticing touch of their bodies moulded together so slickly, in the feel of his mouth exploring her warm, wet skin.

It was only just light when Finch, stirring beside her, woke Blythe the next morning.

'Is it time to get up?' she queried drowsily without opening her eyes, and unconsciously snuggling closer to the inviting warmth of his hard body.

Finch rolled on to his side and pressed a kiss to her bare shoulder. 'For me it is, but you needn't bother. Stay where it's warm for another hour or so. I'll come in and see you before I leave.'

Abrupt realisation had Blythe's eyes flicking open swiftly. 'Oh, that's right, it's the start of the muster, isn't it?' She smiled languidly, and, still cocooned in the contentment created by their lovemaking, without thinking, lifted a finger to trace the bold lines of his face, the firm contours of the mouth that had given her so much pleasure only hours before. 'Do you know when you'll be returning?' she questioned on a soft note.

Catching hold of her hand, Finch caressed each of her fingers leisurely with his lips before pressing a sensuous kiss to her palm. 'Not the exact day, but in just over a week,' he advised huskily.

Blythe inhaled shakily at the sensations he was evoking, and abruptly snapping out of her languorous state, swiftly pulled her hand free. If she wasn't careful he would soon know precisely how she felt about him, and then the last of her defences wuld be lost for ever.

'In other words, I should expect you when I see you,' she surmised in deliberately offhand tones.

As if he sensed her mental withdrawal, Finch's gaze immediately narrowed a little. 'More or less.' There was a short pause. 'And I'd better not hear you've been seen with that snake, Nathan, again either during my absence,' he warned in a roughened voice. Adding speculatively, 'Or maybe I should just arrange for you and Lief to stay with Verna, anyway.'

'Don't you dare!' Blythe flared immediately, rankled by his arbitrary suggestion as well as stung by his continuing distrust. 'I won't be treated as some recalcitrant and unreliable child by you or anyone else, Finch!'

His jaw tightened. 'Then you'd better make certain that bastard doesn't come creeping around again, hadn't you?'

Flashing grey eyes clashed with glinting green. 'And is that why we have sex,' denigratingly phrased on purpose, 'every night? In order to make me pregnant as soon as possible, and so stake *your* claim, once and for all?' Contempt laced her voice.

To her astonishment, and no little confusion, the corners of Finch's mouth suddenly lifted in amusement. 'Whether you become pregnant or not is for you to decide, isn't it? he countered drily.

Blythe's cheeks filled with self-conscious colour, and, flustered, she looked away. It was true, she hadn't taken any precautions against such an occurrence. Because, in reality, she wanted his child? Swallowing, she coerced her gaze back to his and her chin to lift.

'I—well, then I'm surprised you haven't insisted I accompany you, if you doubt me so much,' she huffed to cover her embarrassment.

'I was sure you would prefer to remain with Lief,' he relayed shortly with a dismissive shrug.

Or rather, that was the way *he* preferred it! she amended astringently. Once more, just as Nathan had alleged. Her husband's only real interest in her was as a mother to his nephew.

'Yes, well, it's pleasant to know I do at least have a function that's more to my liking . . . other than providing an outlet for your physical needs,' she gibed with eloquent mockery.

Finch smiled sourly. 'Exactly as I thought!' he clipped out in harsh accents and, throwing back the covers, rose from the bed to begin dressing with tautly controlled movements.

Blythe watched him covertly from beneath her curling lashes. He had taken exception to her taunt about physical needs, she supposed, but despite still considering she had been entitled to make it, conversely, she didn't want them parting with bad feeling between them, and consequently prepared to leave the bed also.

'I said you didn't have to bother to get up,' Finch promptly reminded her curtly—advice she resolutely disregarded as she hurriedly set about donning jeans and a thick sweater. It was their coldest morning to date, she was positive.

'Although I do still happen to be your wife, and since you'll need breakfast before you leave . . .' She spread her hands meaningfully.

'I can make it. I wouldn't want you doing me any favours.'

Blythe pressed her lips together, but refused to allow him to goad her into losing her temper. 'I'm not. I happen to be hungry myself,' she lied. 'So do you want yours now, or just before you leave?'

Momentarily, she thought he meant to rebuff her again, but then, to her relief, he merely flexed a muscular shoulder impassively and acquiesced, 'Now, thanks. I prefer to get moving as soon as the last of the loading's completed.'

With a cursory nod, Blythe made for the kitchen. Soon she had stoked up the fire in the stove, and was grateful for the extra warmth it provided. Later she was to recall ruefully that although it had at least taken the chill from the room, it had done little to warm the atmosphere between Finch and herself.

CHAPTER NINE

'WELL, are you coming or not?' was Nerida's response to Blythe's surprised reaction on finding the other girl visiting her two mornings later.

'C-coming where?' Blythe stammered, frowning.

'To the muster, of course! You did say you'd like to see it, didn't you?'

'Well . . . yes.' Blythe's heart first leapt, and then plunged again. 'B-but how can I? You know I don't ride, and—and then there's Lief to be taken into account as well.'

'Oh, Mum will look after him,' Nerida dismissed that obstacle carelessly with a grin as she seated herself at the kitchen table. 'You know how she dotes on him, and since he feels much the same about her, I can't see him being averse to staying with her.'

'That's true enough,' Blythe was willing to accede, smiling. 'Unfortunately, though,' her expression turned wry, 'that still doesn't endow *me* with the ability to ride.'

'No, well, I was only thinking about that while I was having my fitting yesterday,' the other girl revealed. 'And really, I don't see why you can't come with me today, regardless. I mean, you have to have your first lesson some time, so why not on the way up there? Although it's uphill most of the way, it's not all *that* far from where we leave the trucks. We can take it at an easy pace, and those places where it does get a bit steep you could always walk, or double up behind me. It would at least get you there, and although you couldn't actually take part in the muster, of course, it would at least let you watch some of it. I can lend you whatever clothes and gear you need; we're much of the same size, and I've got just the horse for you. Harmony is as quiet and sure-footed as they come, and she knows all the trails up there like the back of her hand . . . hoof,' she amended with a laugh. 'In fact, I think she was quite dejected at not going this year when Dad and the others left. I'm sure the horses know when the muster's due, and they look forward to it as much as we do.'

Blythe wouldn't have been at all surprised. Finch and his cousins weren't the only ones she had noticed showing signs of restlessness the last month or so. Even the dogs seemed to have sensed the muster was approaching and grown equally restive as well.

'So what do you think of the idea?' Nerida now asked. 'Do you want to give it a go?'

'Oh, yes, I'd love to!' Blythe's response was enthusiastic. Then her face fell, and she chewed at her lip doubtfully. 'But somehow I—I don't think Finch would be of the same mind,' she divulged reluctantly with a diffident shrug.

Nerida's brows arched expressively. 'Why ever not?'

Still unwilling to disclose that her husband hadn't seen fit to even ask if she might like to accompany him, Blythe temporised instead, 'I think he probably considers I'd just be a liability and get in everyone's way.'

Nerida frowned, gazing at her askance. 'Not if I stay with you, though,' she reasoned at length.

'No, but then that wouldn't be fair to you, and in any case he . . .'

'Blythe!' the other girl broke in with wry exasperation. 'Stop making excuses!' Pausing, she looked humorously speculative. 'Or is it just because the two of you have had some sort of argument or other?'

Blythe's breath caught in her throat. 'What makes you think that?' she queried tightly, warily.

'Just the fact that I happened to suggest to Finch the other morning before they left that you might find it lonely with him away, and promptly had my head almost snapped off with the comment that he very much doubted it because you preferred to remain behind,' Nerida relayed drily.

'Oh, that's a lie! He never even . . . well, never mind that!' Blythe cut short her furious words with a snap, even now reluctant to divulge all details. She drew a deep breath, coming to a decision. 'But if that's the case, of course I'll come!' If only to defeat her husband's efforts to have her stay behind! she added to herself.

'Well, let's go, then.' Nerida accepted her sudden change of mind smilingly, and was already starting to her feet. 'We'll check what you have that's suitable to bring with you, and I can provide whatever else you need in the way of stock boots, hat, oilskin, sleeping bag, and so forth.'

Thus, some time before midday—with arrangements made for Verna to look after Lief and the stock—the two girls were well on their way into the mountains. The lower slopes were a forest of ribbon gum, blue gum, stringybark, and thick scrub filled with a variety of wildlife, but the higher they climbed—the rough tracks wandering around and between ridges, along great spurs, sometimes only just clinging to the sides of them, at other times clawing over them—so the vegetation and the trees began to thin until woollybutt and alpine ash predominated.

Then presently, as they reached a small plateau, the last narrow fire trail they had been following came to an end in a clearing where the vehicles the men had used were parked beside on old wooden hut, and halting their own smaller truck next to them, Nerida offloaded their mounts and her two dogs while Blythe set out the lunch Verna had packed for them.

As her companion had predicted, it was much cooler here than in the valley, Blythe noted. The breeze had a distinct chill to it now, the clouds shading the sun altogether on occasion as they floated slowly across the mountain tops above them. The ranges rolled away in serried ranks in every direction, their ridges densely covered in trees that were still dark and green as they awaited their mantle of winter snow, and while they ate their lunch Nerida pointed out the various landmarks; defining the routes through the bush they could follow when driving the cattle up on to the high plains at the start of the · summer, as well as those they took to reach the valley once the muster was concluded.

Their lunch finished, it was time for them to resume their journey, and Blythe approached her first riding lesson in a mixture of anticipation and trepidation. What if she found she didn't like it, or couldn't get the hang of it? she wondered anxiously. Although, as it eventuated, she discovered that, with her mount proving extremely well behaved, and Nerida keeping a close eye on her as well as ensuring they kept to an easy walk, there was very little to dislike or that was unachievable.

At least, that was, while their course was a relatively gradual climb. When they came to those parts where the track became interspersed with rocks and boulders as it rose sharply—and seemingly always with a precipice on one side just waiting for the inattentive, or incompetent!— Blythe immediately put prudence before valour and opted to traverse them on foot, albeit frequently with some considerable panting. The dogs watched these efforts with somewhat bemused expressions on their canine faces, as well they might, Blythe owned ruefully, supposing they had never seen such antics before. It simply strengthened her determination to learn to ride, however, and, she hoped, with almost as much skill and confidence as Nerida displayed, for at times she felt most envious of the deftness and poise with which the other girl instinctively handled her mount, even in the trickiest of situations.

Nevertheless, when they made their way out of yet another gully on to an open, grassed plain and her companion indicated a pocket of snow gums ahead—these trees now having taken over completely from the others—saying that their destination was just the other side of them, Blythe wasn't entirely sorry. She might not have been sore, but her legs and back had begun to ache quite noticeably.

Built in the shelter of a slight rise, the surrounding trees gnarled and twisted into contorted shapes by strong winds and below-freezing temperatures, the Carmodys' hut with its nearby collection of wooden yards, one already containing a number of cattle, was a welcome sight despite being devoid of human occupation at that time of day. It would be late in the afternoon before the men returned. Carrying in the roll that had been strapped to her saddle and which contained her changes of clothing and other few requisites, Blythe glanced interestedly about the structure.

The huge stone fireplace—wide enough to boil water, cook meals, and dry clothing all at the one time—dominated the inside. The floor was of rough, split slabs, what little furniture there was—a trestle table, bench seats, a single cupboard—was also constructed in the same basic fashion, a few stools of cross-cut logs providing extra seating. At one end there were a couple of rough-hewn double bunks, above that a plank sleeping paltform which extended from one wall of the single room to the other. Beneath the bunks were boxes of tinned food, the cupboard filled with flour, tea, sugar, and other packaged goods, while at the other end of the room there was a wire safe containing the meat, the shelves that lined the walls between the two areas filled with an assortment of smaller items and eating utensils.

Outside, an enclosed lean-to kept the horse feed and stacked firewood dry; a tank to collect rainwater from the roof supplementing the spring a hundred yards distant, and the small front veranda providing a protected area for the overnight storage of saddlery. Making use of the latter themselves now after turning their horses into one of the yards, Nerida and Blythe returned inside with armfuls of wood to light the fire and set a billy of water to boil for some tea.

It was nearing dusk when they first heard the men approaching, the ringing crack of stock-whips reaching them before anything else, and

as Blythe followed Nerida out on to the veranda
to await their appearance, she tried to ignore the
fact that her stomach seemed determined to tie
itself in knots at the thought of her coming
meeting with Finch. Just what would his reaction
be to her presence?

It took an increasingly anxious while until she
found out, for even after the men finally arrived,
the cattle they drove before them still had to be
yarded, the horses unsaddled and rubbed down
before being turned into their own yard and fed.
Following that there was a brief dousing with
cold water from the spring—the same as the two
girls had done an hour or so before—and only
then was a move towards the hut made.

'I hope that smoke spiralling from the chimney
signifies the tea's already made and the dinner's
on,' Brent quipped to his sister as he bounded on
to the veranda ahead of the others. 'It was my
turn to prepare the meal tonight.' Then, peering
into the darkening gloom, 'Who's that with you?'

'Just Blythe,' supplied Nerida wryly.

'Oh—sorry. I didn't recognise you.' He smiled
at the younger girl now as he deposited his saddle
and blanket beside the wall before continuing on
inside.

Well, at least he had accepted her readily
enough, mused Blythe gratefully, but she still
waited tensely, her eyes glued to her husband's
tall figure as the others approached together.

This time, however, Nerida apparently decided
to prevent any such further confusion and took it

upon herself to announce so that all could hear, 'I brought Blythe along with me. She decided she'd like to come too.'

The response from her immediate family was much the same as Brent's had been; slight surprise followed by equable acceptance before they also dropped their saddles near the wall and disappeared inside. All the same, it was Finch's reaction Blythe was waiting for, and she was glad Nerida had tactfully accompanied her father into the hut when Finch didn't immediately say anything, but merely regarded her with narrowed eyes while he also unburdened himself of his gear and then turned to face her—or should that have been confront her? speculated Blythe nervously—with his hands resting squarely on his lean hips.

'OK, so what the hell are you doing here?' he demanded flatly without preamble.

Blyte raised a deprecating shoulder. 'I—well, you heard what Nerida said, and—and since Verna was more than prepared to look after Lief, I was sure you would prefer being able to keep me under close scrutiny considering how much you distrust me!' Traces of sarcasm coupled with bitterness surfaced in her tone. 'While in return, I can do the same to you!'

'Meaning?'

'Well, there are other females who participate in the muster, aren't there?' Others apart from Delvene, that was! 'I wouldn't like to think your determination to have me stay behind was so you could sneak off with one of them behind *my* back!'

Finch's mouth curved at that, but whether in amusement or disdain the lighting was too poor for her to tell. 'Well, apart from the fact that during the day there's nothing much on my mind apart from cattle, and at night . . . these huts don't exactly allow for any privacy, as you can see, so even if I did feel that way inclined there wouldn't be much chance of success, and particularly since all those females, including Delvene,' inserted as if he could read her mind, 'happen to be mustering on other leases,' he mocked.

'Oh! Well, I wasn't to know that!' she excused herself defensively. 'You certainly never want out of your way to tell me anything about what goes on here!' Resentment began to edge back into her voice.

'You never asked!' Finch snapped back promptly. 'Anyway, just what do you mean by *my* determination to have you remain behind?'

'Well, wasn't it? You certainly never even asked if I'd like to come, or—or to participate!' Unbidden tears welled into her eyes.

Finch dragged a hand roughly around the back of his neck. 'How could you?' There was a hint of irony amid the exasperation. 'You can't even ride!'

'Although that didn't stop me from getting here today on horseback . . . because Nerida, at least, was prepared to be helpful!' Blythe retorted pointedly. 'In any case, you couldn't even be bothered to ask if I wanted to learn!'

'Because if that was what you wanted, all you had to do was say so!'

Blythe shook her head in rebuttal. 'How could I?' she choked. 'I—I'm just here to look after Lief. The farm and everything on it is yours! I don't have any—rights to anything!' Tears spilled on to her cheeks now and she brushed them away embarrassedly.

'For God's sake! You bear my name!' Finch rasped savagely, ripping his hat from his head and slapping it forcefully against a muscular thigh. 'What's that, if not giving you the right to whatever I own?'

Blythe caught her lower lip between her teeth, shaking her head. 'You don't understand,' she whispered miserably, and already discomfited by the humiliating thought that those inside might have been able to overhear them, stepped blindly from the veranda to seek refuge in the descending darkness beyond.

'No, I bloody don't understand!' conceded Finch in growling accents behind her. 'So maybe you'd better explain, huh?'

Explain that if they had married for love instead of convenience, she would have felt quite differently about it? Explain that if he had cared for her, she wouldn't have felt she was only there from necessity?

'There's nothing to—explain,' she turned to deny unsteadily. 'It—it's just how I feel, that's all.'

'So how *do* you feel, Blythe?' A certain nuance in his tone had her eyes widening warily as she watched his inexorable approach, seemingly held fast by the probing green gaze that locked with hers, and which was far more visible now that they had left the shadowed veranda.

'I've just t-told you,' she just managed to get out protectively.

Finch drew an audible breath. 'I meant . . . about us . . . our relationship! Because that is the cause of all of this, isn't it?'

Blythe swallowed heavily and, dragging her gaze from his at last, bent her head. 'I thought it was about my attending the muster,' she evaded, and gasped when an inflexible hand forced her face up to his again.

'Don't be provoking, sweetheart!' Finch warned on a roughened note. 'I'm already having enough trouble controlling my instincts, as it is!' Suddenly, an unexpectedly bitter twist caught at his lips. 'But then where you're concerned, I guess that's always been my problem, hasn't it?'

'I don't know what you mean,' she whispered hesitantly in puzzlement.

'Oh, don't give me that!' he rasped scornfully. 'You know only too damned well what you do to me!' He shook his head in disbelief. 'Even now, as tired and dirty as I am, all I can think of is making love to you until you haven't the strength to fight me any more!'

Blythe trembled. 'Because I came here when

you didn't want me to?'

'Because you came when I didn't think *you* wanted to! Because you'll never know what it took to leave you behind!'

'Because you thought I'd be seeing Nathan again,' she deduced dejectedly, her spirits sinking again after they had fleetingly started to rise.

'Partly,' Finch owned. He paused, beginning to caress her cheek with the back of his hand. 'But mostly, because I didn't want to be parted from you.'

'You didn't . . . ?' hardly daring to believe.

He shook his head.

Again a quiver of almost unbearable hope ran through Blythe, and she unknowingly moved closer to him. 'Why not, Finch?' she breathed tautly, her eyes clinging to his. 'Why didn't you?'

'Damn you! You know why not!' he groaned, catching her close against his chest. 'Because I haven't been able to get you out of my mind since the first time I met you! Because not a day goes past that I don't fall just a little deeper in love with you!'

Blythe thought her heart would burst with happiness, and with no reason for restraint any more, she threw her arms around his neck, holding him tightly. 'Oh, Finch, I love you so much too!' she declared fervently, and for some time no more words were necessary as their lips met hungrily, and satisfyingly erased any lingering doubts either of them might have had . . .

*   *   *

'At last!' said Finch in marked satisfaction, tugging Blythe down on to his lap as he lounged on the sofa in front of the crackling fire. 'The thought of holding you like this has been on my mind for days.'

Blythe smiled and nodded, her arms linking about his neck, her mouth responding with equal ardour to the pressure of his as he kissed her with devastating thoroughness.

It was their first night home after the muster, and with Lief now in bed, they finally had the privacy they had both been yearning for. Not that Blythe would have wanted to miss the muster, for she had found it fascinating. It had opened a whole new world to her as she watched the others slip into what was evidently a long-practised routine.

Everyone had taken their turn at whatever work needed to be done, whether it was lighting fires, cooking dinner and breakfast, making tea, feeding the horses and dogs, staying behind to keep watch on the already mustered stock when they were let out of the yards to graze, or spending ten hours a day in the saddle—oblivious to the weather that on occasion had drenched, warmed, or chilled to the bone—searching out the cattle from the grassy plains, wooded slopes, and scrub-filled gullies.

But now it was over for another year, the stock returned to their paddocks awaiting the forthcoming sales, and winter, the quietest time on the property, was almost upon them.

'I'm thinking a honeymoon would be in order,' Finch murmured huskily as his lips roved across Blythe's creamy cheek to her ear. Lifting his head, he gave a beguiling grin. 'Somewhere hot, for preference, so there wouldn't be the need for all these damn clothes.' His expression turned ruefully frustrated as he slid his hands under her sweater and encountered the blouse she was wearing beneath.

Blythe smiled, then eyed him back in assumed affront. 'Are you only interested in my body, sir?' she chided.

Finch's face sobered, and freeing his hands he cupped her face with them instead. 'As delicious as it is, my sweet, I've always wanted more than just that from you,' he disclosed in deepened tones. 'I wanted your love, your mind, your soul even, from the time I made up my mind I was going to marry you.' His lips twitched. 'And that was long before Lief conveniently provided the means to achieve that end, I might add.'

'You mean you wanted to marry me, even if Lief hadn't said he would only stay if I did?' she queried in wide-eyed astonishment.

'My love, he was merely an excuse. I wanted you any way I could get you, and I *was* determined to have you, make no mistake about that!' He brushed his mouth sensuously across her parted lips. 'I did say once that it wasn't gratitude I wanted from you . . . remember?'

'But—but that was the first day Lief and I arrived here!' she gasped.

Finch smiled, heart-shakingly. 'I knew what I'd been waiting for when it finally arrived, sweetheart,' he drawled significantly.

Blythe gave an incredulous shake of her head. 'While I thought you only married me because of Lief,' she lamented. 'If only I'd realised earlier!'

'I'm surprised you didn't that day I discovered you with Nathan,' he put forward wryly. 'Hell, I was so damned jealous I could have killed him with my bare hands!'

Blythe bit at her lip in remembrance. 'Oh, Finch, I'm sorry,' she said contritely. 'I knew I shouldn't have agreed to meet him—I felt guilty about it the whole way there, in fact—but when he phoned me and suggested it, I . . . well, he made me feel as if I couldn't make a decision for myself any more if I couldn't just meet him for a talk. And that's all I went for, Finch, honestly . . . just to talk,' she impressed on him anxiously. 'It never occurred to me that he would lose his self-control to such an extent as to actually kiss me in public! He never had before!' She bent her head. 'In any event, I had hoped you wouldn't ever learn of it because I envisaged being home again before you returned, only . . .' she sighed regretfully, 'it didn't quite work out that way.' Her eyes lifted quizzically to his. 'How come you did arrive back so early that day, Finch . . . and apparently knew where to find me?'

His eyes darkened, his hands beginning to smooth caressingly up and down her wool-covered arms, making her long for the feel of them against her skin. 'I returned early because I wanted to see you, because I'd missed you so much,' he revealed thickly, and she unconsciously pressed closer to him. 'As for discovering where you were . . .' He gave a small shrug. 'When Jarred pointed out that your car was gone, I phoned Price and Verna, but as they hadn't seen you, we drove down to the shop in Yuroka to find out if they'd happened to see you go past. They had, although to where they'd had no idea until they happened to be speaking on the phone to someone who mentioned in passing that they'd seen you in Omeo.' His mouth tilted crookedly. 'News travels fast in a small community.'

'Evidently,' she responded with a half-smile, her fingers moving to tangle within his dark hair. 'Although no matter how unnerving it may have been at the time, that afternoon did at least succeed in teaching me one thing.'

'And that was . . . ?'

'Just who my heart really did belong to,' she confessed softly, and his descending mouth satisfactorily prevented her from continuing for some time. 'Oh, I'd known for a while that you attracted me,' she went on when she was at last able. 'Right from our first meeting you'd had an unsettling effect on me. But when we made love that afternoon, I couldn't deny my feelings any longer, and I knew then that you were the only man I wanted, would ever want, in my life.'

'Oh, love!' Finch groaned raggedly, his mouth finding hers unerringly again, and gathering her into his arms he rose lithely upright with her cradled against him. 'How did I ever survive before you came along? I love you to distraction, and I promise you, this night is going to be the real start of our marriage.'

Happier than she had ever thought it possible to be, Blythe pressed her lips to his tanned throat as he carried her into their bedroom. 'Although only the first of many such nights,' she forecast eloquently.

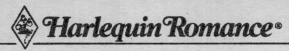
Harlequin Romance®

Coming Next Month

2995   SOME ENCHANTED EVENING   Jenny Arden
Eve has to admit that Zack Thole is persistent, and wickedly
handsome, but she is almost committed to Greg and has no
intention of being carried away by moonlight and madness. Yet
Zack can be very persuasive....

2996   LORD OF THE LODGE   Miriam MacGregor
Lana comes to New Zealand's Kapiti coast to find the father she's
never known, having discovered he works at the Leisure Lodge
guest house. Owner Brent Tremaine, however, completely
misinterprets her interest in his employee. Surely he can't
be jealous?

2997   SHADES OF YESTERDAY   Leigh Michaels
Necessity forces Courtney to approach old Nate Winslow for help.
After all, Nate owes her something—her mother had said so—
though Courtney doesn't know what. So it annoys her that his son
Jeff regards her as an undesirable scrounger!

2998   LOVE ON A STRING   Celia Scott
Bryony not only designs and makes kites, she loves flying them—
and Knucklerock Field is just the right spot. When Hunter Green
declares his intention to turn it into a helicopter base, it's like a
declaration of war between them!

2999   THE HUNGRY HEART   Margaret Way
Liane has steered clear of Julian Wilde since their divorce. But when
Jonathon, her small stepson, needs her help, she just can't stay
away—even though it means facing Julian again. After all, it isn't as
if he still loved her.

3000   THE LOST MOON FLOWER
Bethany Campbell

"Whitewater, I want you." These three desperate words not only
move lone hunter Aaron Whitewater to guide Josie through the
treacherous mountains of a tiny Hawaiian island to retrieve a
priceless stolen panda, they prove dangerously prophetic....

Available in August wherever paperback books are sold, or
through Harlequin Reader Service:

In the U.S.
901 Fuhrmann Blvd.
P.O. Box 1397
Buffalo, N.Y. 14240-1397

In Canada
P.O. Box 603
Fort Erie, Ontario
L2A 5X3

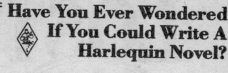

Have You Ever Wondered If You Could Write A Harlequin Novel?

Here's great news—Harlequin is offering a series of cassette tapes to help you do just that. Written by Harlequin editors, these tapes give practical advice on how to make your characters—and your story— come alive. There's a tape for each contemporary romance series Harlequin publishes.

Mail order only

All sales final

This is a work of fiction. All the characters and events portrayed in this book are fictitious, and any resemblance to real people or events is purely coincidental.

KINSHIP WITH THE STARS

Cover art by Brian Waugh

A Tor Book
Published by Tom Doherty Associates, Inc.
49 West 24th Street
New York, N.Y. 10010

ISBN: 0-812-51814-4

First edition: October 1991

Printed in the United States of America

0 9 8 7 6 5 4 3 2

POUL ANDERSON
KINSHIP WITH THE STARS

A TOM DOHERTY ASSOCIATES BOOK
NEW YORK

Recent Tor books by Poul Anderson

ALIGHT IN THE VOID
THE BOAT OF A MILLION YEARS
EXPLORATIONS
THE LONG NIGHT
THE LONGEST VOYAGE
NO TRUCE WITH KINGS
THE SATURN GAME
THE SHIELD OF TIME
STARSHIP
THE TIME PATROL